The Good,
the Bat,
and the Ugly

The Good,
the Bat,
and the Ugly

Paul Magrs

Illustrations by Alan Snow

Atheneum Books for Young Readers
New York London Toronto Sydney

Atheneum Books for Young Readers
An imprint of Simon & Schuster Children's Publishing Division
1230 Avenue of the Americas
New York, New York 10020

First published in Great Britain in 2003 by Simon & Schuster UK Ltd

The text of this book is set in Galliard.
The illustrations are rendered in pen and ink.

Manufactured in the United States of America

First U.S. Edition, 2004
10 9 8 7 6 5 4 3 2 1

Library of Congress Cataloging-in-Publication Data
Magrs, Paul, 1969–
The good, the bat, and the ugly / Paul Magrs.—1st ed.
p.   cm.
Summary: When famous puppets of British television are murdered, everyone
suspects thirteen-year-old Jason's father, a bitter, forgotten puppeteer, of
committing the grisly acts.
ISBN 0-689-87019-1
[1. Puppets—Fiction. 2. Fathers and sons—Fiction. 3. England—Fiction.
4. Humorous stories.] I. Title.
PZ7 .M2757 Han 2004
[Fic]—dc22   2003062789

for Louise and Mark

with thanks to:
Joy Foster, Gladys Johnston, Nicola Creegan,
Lynne Heritage, Paula Kipling, Pete Courtie,
Jon and Antonia Rolfe, Alicia Stubbersfield, Siri Reynolds, Brigid
Robinson, Sara Maitland, Amanda Reynolds,
Richard Klein, Lucie Scott, Reuben Lane,
Georgina Hammick, Maureen Duffy, Shena Mackay,
Patrick Gale, Patricia Duncker, Val Striker, Michele Roberts,
Marina Mackay, Stewart Sheargold, Victor Sage,
Lorna Sage, Stephen Cole, Penelope Webber,
Stephen Hornby, Jo Moses, Bridget O'Connor,
Peter Straughan, Jenny Newman, Melvin Burgess,
Neil Gaiman, Jac Rayner, Justin Richards, Tiffany
Murray and Larry, Carol Ann Johnson, Margaret Hope,
Jon Cook, Wayne Clews, Jake Huntley, Oliver Emmanuel,
Ann Brodie and, of course, Jeremy Hoad.

One

I hate it when people ask me what I want to be when I grow up. When Mam or Dad come out with this question I flush bright red and I grit my teeth and I don't say anything.

How am I supposed to know? I'm only thirteen.

They're weird for asking, is what I think. But they think *I'm* weird because I ought to know already what I want to be. They cluck their tongues and they stare at me across the living room or down the dining table.

It's like they're thinking that something is wrong with me. But really, I think it would be weirder to know exactly what I was going to turn out like.

I don't have any firm ideas or plans. Plans are for losers. Plans are for weirdos.

"You want to try out computers, our Jason?"

That's my mam. That's what she always says at this point in the conversation. "They're the thing of the future, you know. That's where we're all going. Anyone of your age who doesn't know his way around a computer . . . well, they won't be anything. Not in the future."

My mam likes to think of herself as very modern. She's very keen on the future and being all equipped for it. She's slim and up-to-the-minute and always dressed in what she thinks are the latest fashions. On the particular day I'm talking about—during one of these talks we were always having—she was wearing a spangly blue catsuit, ropes of false pearls around her neck, and two false fairy wings strapped to her back. This was something she'd seen modeled on morning TV, which is where she gets all her fashion ideas from.

It's where she gets most of her ideas about everything.

What I've never understood is that if Mam is so keen on the future and all things modern, why she ever got together with a man like my dad. I mean, he's ancient. He's a skinny old man whose breath stinks of chewing tobacco and Fisherman's Friends, and he's at least three times the age of my mam.

"Oh, you don't understand the mysterious workings of love," Mam says when I ask her why she saddled herself with such an old bloke. "You're only thirteen. One day you'll see. You'll understand love when you grow up."

What I *do* understand is that my dad is evil. Really, truly evil. I mean, he was always a bit short-tempered and nasty, but just lately he's been worse than ever. Ever since that fall he'd taken in the attic when he was clearing through his old stuff. He'd hit his head and come downstairs in a stinking mood that had clung around him for weeks.

He sits at the head of our dinner table during the silent, ominous, frugal meals we have and he gives off this terrible atmosphere. It's like a horrible smell that takes over our whole house. When we're having dinner it's like the crockery is clinking in trepidation and the knives and forks and spoons are tinkling in fear. The gravy and the custard always grow a thick skin when they stand out on the table, the milk curdles in the jug and if we're having a chicken, say, it looks like it wants to get up and fling itself on the carving knife in order to make sure it's quite safely dead.

Mealtimes are especially awful at our house. No one ever comes to visit and you can understand why. It's only ever me, Mam, and Dad. Sat there.

Today we were having broccoli, which had been boiled till it had gone yellow and mushy, with raw onions whole and rolling about on our plates. This was because Mam had watched something about healthier eating on telly.

"This is awful muck," Dad grumbled, stabbing at his broccoli.

We didn't dare say anything back.

The thing about my dad that you have to understand is that he used to have millions of fans—millions of fans who knew him as Frank. I just know him as Dad, but my mam calls him Frank, of course.

He used to be known to all those people back when he had his own TV show on Saturday nights. This was twenty years ago or something. Prehistory. Now everyone's forgotten about him.

This is one of the reasons my dad has turned evil. Well, that's not strictly true. The bump on the head in the attic didn't help much and he was always a bit evil really. But, as Mam says, disappointment, obscurity and neglect have done his head in more than anything and made him much, much worse.

And we get the flak for that.

The fact that nobody stops and recognizes him in the

street and goes, "Hold on a minute! It's . . . it's Frank Lurcher, isn't it? The TV star?"

And he could say, "Bugger off. I've no time for fans today." But he would be secretly pleased as he stomped off. That's how he used to go on, Mam says.

Back then he used to have reporters from the *Radio Times* asking him things like how he'd be spending Christmas Day this year. "Quietly at home, with my lovely family in my luxurious home. We're having a giant bat stuffed with nettles, and oysters for dinner. We're very traditional." Mam showed me a scrapbook of clippings of this kind of thing. There's Dad, still old, but twenty years younger than the ancient man he is now.

No one asks Dad anything anymore. No one cares.

Mam says that when they used to interview him, he only ever said nasty things anyway. He went on this radio show, *Desert Island Discs*, when he was still famous (hanging on to fame by the skin of his manky yellow teeth), and the songs he picked for them to play were horrible things like "The Funeral March" and "The Birdie Song."

Even all those years ago, Frank Lurcher was never a very popular celebrity.

Of course he still carries on like he's the most famous and

important person in the world. That's what he's like with us, at home. In the real world outside, no one even turns their head when he passes by and if he acts self-important and rude they just think he's crazy. But secretly, at home, me and Mam live with someone who thinks he's as famous as the Queen.

We live in something like fear. There's always a tremor in my mam's voice.

It was there that afternoon, as she went on about how I ought to get into computers.

"So that's what you want for Christmas, is it, then, Jason? A great big whopping computer of the flashiest kind, hmm? With a printer and modems and all that malarkey, eh? Just so's you can become an expert and a whizkid and make an absolute fortune and travel all over the world?"

Mam puts on this bright, brittle voice and I know she worries that I'll never get away from this dark, damp house and my dad's evil shadow.

I wanted to say no, not really. I didn't want a computer. I never get on well with electronic or mechanical things. They always seem to break apart in my hands or go wrong some- how. I get quite nervous about things that can go wrong. I don't know why. Everyone at school seems to be fine with things like that. With the machines they use in the machine shop in metalwork, with the computers in the computer room that they use in computer studies. Whenever I even touch those things they seem to go haywire; they crash or burn or go off with a bang.

I'm used to the idea of being useless. That's what my dad tells me I am.

Whatever my parents were going to get me for Christmas wouldn't help me. I'm bound to be useless all my life.

But I smiled weakly at Mam. It's always best not to say much at mealtimes.

Dad cleared his throat loudly and with a vile rattle. "The kid doesn't want a computer thing," he said. "I don't hold with machines like that, taking over the world."

We had heard this speech before. It was the one about the end-of-decent-civilization-as-we-know-it.

"What they do," he was going on, "is make everything much too complicated. Everything is run by computers! It's the end of decent civilization as we know it! What's wrong with hands, eh? What's wrong with proper manual work? Even primitive man in his caves could make things with his hands! He could make fire! He could paint his cave walls! What can we do, eh? Bugger all! That's what!"

Dad's voice always gets higher- and higher-pitched when he launches into these rants of his. I looked down at my untouched broccoli and raw onion.

"Why, I go into the bank or the betting shop on High Street and I end up having to argue with the staff because they can't do anything! They're hopeless! They depend on their machines too much! All that bleeping and blinking! Drives you crackers, in the end, all that. They can't think for themselves! They don't have any initiative!"

Dad tends to go on like this for a while when he's in the mood. The upshot is that he thinks the world is in a pretty poor state. Everything changed, he believes, the very day that the director-general of the company that used to make his TV show decided to take him off the air. Ever since then the world has been going rapidly downhill.

"Look at checkout girls in supermarkets!" he shrieked at us, waving his knife in the air. "They can't even add in their heads anymore! They just pass your food under a red laser eye, and it goes KERPLUNK KERPLUNK KERPLUNK all over the place and adds your bill up for them! And it gets it wrong! It probably overcharges you pounds and pounds! It's ridiculous! And not very nice either. Laser beams! Going all over the place! All over your groceries! You could be sent blind!"

Dad was a bit short of breath by now.

"Anyway," he gasped, when he had calmed down a little, put down his knife and combed back the hair that had come unstuck from his bald patch. "I've got a much, much better idea for what young Jason should be given for his Christmas present this year. Yes, a much better present. Much better for our Jason than a stinky, mind-sucking computer . . ."

Dad's voice was like dead leaves crackling. Suddenly I felt a shiver down my back.

My mam darted a worried sideways glance at Dad. His stringy, greasy remnants of hair were flapping at the sides of his head in excitement.

We knew something bad was coming.

Mam swallowed hard on a tough bit of onion, as if she knew exactly what *kind* of bad thing was coming.

I watched Dad lick his thin, purple lips.

"It is time . . . ," he began grandly, "that the boy faced up to . . . his destiny."

Destiny? I thought.

Mam's face had turned white. "D-destiny, Frank? Oh, surely not . . ." Her beautifully manicured, skinny hands were shaking. She put them down flat on the tablecloth to keep them steady. "Surely, Frank, you can't mean . . ."

The old man's eyes were burning a horrible orange, like two golden fag ends of malice.

He said, "At last . . . it is time!"

I had stopped breathing by now.

Dad stood up and gazed into the distance, out of the bay window, through the net curtains. It was like he was in a trance.

"It is time for the boy to learn . . . the family trade! You can't keep him from it any longer, Eileen. You can't stand between your weakling, useless son and his ultimate destiny!"

"Oh, Frank . . . ," Mam said quietly, and then looked at me strangely, almost wonderingly.

"We are going to buy him," Dad shrieked, "his first puppet!"

Mam slumped back in her dining chair. She looked utterly defeated.

And just for the moment I didn't know what to think.

Two

It was never for himself that my dad was famous. Oh, he had had his own Saturday tea-time series all right, but it wasn't really his. He used to get into the *Radio Times* and on *Desert Island Discs* and everything, but it wasn't about him that the public at home really wanted to know.

The person they really wanted to know about was Tolstoy, his talking, long-eared bat.

His scraggy, filthy, bad-tempered, foul-mouthed, matted, greasy, long-eared bat.

If it hadn't been for Tolstoy, my dad would never have

been on the telly. No one would have watched him. No one would have cared. And Dad knows it.

And nowadays Dad and Tolstoy aren't even on speaking terms. They haven't talked to each other in over twenty years. Their partnership has been dissolved and Tolstoy is idling his time in a chest up in our attic, quite lifeless, almost forgotten.

They'll never be seen together in public again. No more Frank Lurcher and his talking long-eared best friend, the bat. They'll never sing another rasping, vile duet; never engage in witty, sniping repartee; and they'll never again gang up together to make a fool out of this week's special guest.

Never again. Nowadays—actually, for as long as I can remember—the whole topic of glove puppets and puppetry has been out of bounds and forbidden round our house. I've grown up scared to even mention anything to do with glove puppets or marionettes, generally for fear for incurring Dad's wrath.

That's why I was so shocked, that lunchtime in the middle of December, to hear Dad suddenly announce this business of the Christmas-present-of-destiny.

My very own puppet!

Learning the family trade!

I couldn't help feeling that it all spelled bad news. I just had to take one look at my mam's face to see that. It would mean bad news for the whole Lurcher family, but worse news for me in particular.

My dad had been seized by a weird manic energy.

He leaped arthritically into action, out of his chair at the head of our table, and the next thing was he was shouting for his overcoat and his snowboots. Mam went dashing to help him prepare himself. Dad was causing a palaver in the hallway, and he yelled at me that I should get wrapped up warm too, because the two of us were going into town.

Immediately. No messing about.

We were going to pick out and buy my Christmas present right that minute, that very afternoon.

We were going to the Marionette Emporium, though I'd never heard of such a place. It was round the back of the arcade apparently, in the tangle of dark streets where I wasn't allowed to go alone.

"We have to strike while the iron's hot!" squawked Dad, yanking on a ratty old scarf.

Mam's eyes were wide and pleading. "Do as he says!" she was telling me silently, her fake fairy wings quivering at her back. "Don't cause a fuss. You know what your old dad's like . . ."

I got up and obediently started getting ready to go into town with Dad. I fetched my wellies from where they were drying out on newspaper in the kitchen. It was strange, the idea of shopping with my dad. I usually went with Mam. Dad hates going out anywhere and tries to do it as little as possible. "There's nothing for me out there," is his usual complaint. "Not out there in the horrible world outside . . ."

We caught the bus at the end of our street. We live in a forgotten, shady cul-de-sac of old and lonely-looking houses. Our home is the most dilapidated and the most gloomy semi-detached home on the street. It's shrouded over by immense, dark, shabby yew trees, as if to put off strangers coming anywhere near or, perhaps, to help prevent its inhabitants from ever getting out. I looked back at the dark house, though, and wished I was still inside, as my stiff-legged Dad trudged ahead of me through the snow. He was grumbling to himself.

We had to wait a little while at the bus stop. A middle-aged woman with an immense tartan shopping bag and a prim mouth smiled at us and said good afternoon. I recognized her as the woman who lived three doors down from us. I didn't know her name.

My dad glared at her, as if he couldn't believe how rude she was being, addressing us out of the blue like that. "Harlot!" he hissed at her, and she flinched in shock.

Luckily, the bus came along just then.

We've never had our own car. My dad won't drive because

he says that everyone else is an abysmal driver and shouldn't be allowed on the roads. Also, his hands have always been his livelihood and he wouldn't endanger them by putting them on the steering wheel of a car among a whole pack of maniacs. The bus, he says, is quite good enough for anywhere we might want to go.

But the only thing about buses, he started telling me then, as we struggled down the overcrowded gangway looking for a seat, is the common rabble you are forced to mix with on public transport.

"Look at them!" he cackled, as if no one else could hear. "Look at this terrible scruffy bunch!"

My ears were burning with shame as we finally found a seat together.

"Oh, it's unbearable," Dad said. "Nasty people with double incontinence, I'm sure, and ghastly pets and vile screaming children . . ."

He started looking out of the window then, at the streets going by, and his complaints petered out abruptly, as if all the strength had drained from him.

I was left alone with my thoughts for a while as the bus slipped and skidded on the banked-up snow on the roads into town.

My own puppet! I thought. And now I found I couldn't

repress a moment of shivery pleasure at the idea. What kind of animal would it be? What would I call it? What personality would it have? And would I get my own TV show, like Dad?

But, I thought . . . I can't have any talent in that direction. I won't be able to master all the technical skills that you need to be a first-class puppeteer. On the few occasions when Dad had been able to bring himself to talk about the past, he made it clear how terribly difficult and well-nigh impossible it was to be a convincing puppet master. I'll never be half the puppeteer he once was. And wasn't it always Dad who was telling me how clumsy and useless I was? So how could he expect me to learn such a nimble and noble art?

I'd never be able to move the puppet's mouth in time to the words. I'd never be able to give it real expression and life. All the mysteries that Dad goes on about—the real mystique of ventriloquism . . . How would I ever learn to put on different voices and be able to throw them and make it look as if my own lips weren't moving? I find it hard enough to speak up and talk in my own voice. I'd never be able to do it! I'd die of shame . . . or my dad would kill me.

The most awful, difficult, impossibly bleak future was suddenly rising and opening up in front of me aboard the chilly bus as we trundled into the town center.

I was heading towards a rendezvous with fate. And it was

my fate to spend my life with one hand shoved up a stuffed animal, trying to make it answer back realistically when I talked to it. All for the amusement of others.

And to think, only that morning, I'd had no inkling of my destiny. Only that morning I'd been in the blissful position of not knowing what my future would bring. Mam had tried pushing me towards computers and the world of the future, but that hadn't seemed very likely. She had also once tried to get me interested in the idea of becoming a celebrity interior designer. She liked those TV shows where the interior designers do up people's front rooms so that the owners don't even recognize them. I wasn't very keen on that either.

But bless Mam anyway. It strikes me now that she kept putting these different ideas-for-the-future my way in order to save me from this fate of having to have my own glove puppet.

Having to spend my life with my arm up a fake long-eared bat, or a parrot or a monkey. Life is so unfair.

As our bus brought us closer to the shops, I found myself suddenly brave enough to tap Dad on the arm and ask him something that had been bugging me.

"But, Dad! You tried all of this before, didn't you? You tried to pass on the gift and the teaching of the noble art! And it went wrong last time, didn't it? When you tried it with Barry!"

17

Barry is my older brother. He's quite a lot older than me. We never talk about Barry.

For a second there was the most terrible, heart-stopping silence between us.

Then the old man's head swung round and his voice came out very quietly and very low in his wattled throat. His lips hardly budged as he growled back at me.

"You know better than to mention your brother's name in my presence, Jason. You know fine well that we never even say the name of that . . . diabolical traitor!"

And that was the end of the matter. I gulped.

At that moment the bus squealed to an icy halt at our stop, bang in the middle of the busy, tinseled, slushy High Street.

Three

When we hit the bustling street I realized that I wasn't sure exactly where we were going. The Marionette Emporium was a mysterious place, hidden away somewhere that only real puppeteers knew about. Dad, of course, knew precisely where we were headed and he was leading the way through the crowd with his beaky, cold-looking nose thrust out ahead of him. He was cutting an aggressive swathe through the afternoon shoppers, who were clutching their heavy carrier bags and parcels and shuffling away at his approach.

I found myself apologizing to those strays Dad was shoving out of the way with his bony elbows. My dad is one of those old people who think they can behave however they like, pushing into queues and shouting at people. He yells things like, "I fought in two world wars for the likes of you lot!" in busy places, though, as I know, this isn't at all true. Dad never fought in any wars at all. Dad has also been known to bellow, "I used to be an extremely well-known television personality, you know!" Which is true—though when he shouts this, the harried passers-by tend to look at him as though he's crazy.

That afternoon, he was keeping his yelling to a strict

minimum, intent as he was on taking me to the Marionette Emporium. Well, he was relatively quiet until we happened by the main window display of the Megastore.

At that point, right in front of the video store's window, Dad stood stock still with horror. He jabbed an accusatory finger at the dead center of the festive display.

"What," he shrieked, spittle flying out of his twisted, toothless mouth, "what do you suppose is the meaning of that!"

His eyes were bulging out of his skull-like head and if he had had any proper hair, I was sure it would have been standing up on end by now.

"What is the meaning of this . . . travesty?"

The first thing I thought was that it was a pretty lavish window display that the video Megastore had put on. It seemed to involve a whole load of furry, grinning animals staring out of the huge plate-glass window. They were waving at the window shoppers from the middle of what appeared to be a Winter Wonderland, complete with tinsel, holly and fake polystyrene snow. There was an ostrich, a rabbit, a pink poodle and several bears. It was a funny and Christmassy display, all in all, and I was sure it hadn't been designed to provoke the kind of fury that Dad was now exhibiting.

He was jumping up and down on the slippery pavement

outside the shop. "Those vicious, conniving bastards!" he screamed, turning a livid beetroot color.

I grasped his bony arm. "Dad! Don't! You're showing yourself up!"

Dad squawked. "Showing myself up! Showing myself up! I'll show you showing myself up, young fella-me-lad!"

With that he stopped jumping up and down in fury and flung himself into the noisy and overcrowded Megastore, where they were playing ear-splitting dance music that was sure to make Dad's mood even worse. Shoppers were walking up and down the aisles with piles of CDs and videos and boxed sets of all kinds of things.

I still couldn't see what had been so offensive about the seasonal window dressing. It had consisted of a whole load of stuffed animals and a large friendly sign: REMEMBER US?

Before dashing into the Megastore to see what further bother my demented dad might be causing, I stood for a second and read the rest of the sign in the window.

REMEMBER US? WE WERE THE ANIMAL CHUMS OF YOUR YOUTH! WE WERE ALL YOUR FAVORITE FURRY FRIENDS FROM CHILDREN'S TV ALL THOSE YEARS AGO!

CATCH US NOW ON VIDEO! NEW SPE-
CIAL VIDEO AND DVD COLLECTIONS OF
ALL OUR GREATEST TV MOMENTS!!!
AVAILABLE HERE!

When I looked a little closer at the smiling, waving animals I saw that they were, in fact, lifelike facsimiles of very
famous TV puppets of bygone days . . . all of them clumped
and ganged together as if they were firm friends enjoying a bit
of Christmas revelry. All of them seemed very pleased indeed
to be released and available on video tape and DVD.

There was one notable absence, though.

And that was what had got Dad so worked up so quickly.

That was why he'd been screaming at the Megastore window and calling names at the top of his raspy voice.

There was no sign—not a single sign—of Tolstoy the
long-eared bat.

Not the slightest whiff of long-eared bat anywhere in
that display.

It was as if Tolstoy had been wiped right out of the fondly
remembered TV past.

I shuddered. Now there really would be trouble.

I took a deep breath and followed my apoplectic dad into
the unsuspecting shop.

This was all we needed. On a day that was already so fraught and complicated and weird. On a day when the very subject of puppets and famousness had already taken on such a peculiar tinge.

When I managed to catch up with Dad, I found him haranguing a young and already-harassed member of staff who was wearing a Megastore T-shirt and carrying a stack of at least 200 DVDs.

"Who is responsible?" Dad was screaming. "Who is responsible for that . . . blasphemy in your window?"

The sales assistant with the tower of DVDs looked rather worried at this. Maybe he thought Dad belonged to a religious cult. "Do you mean our display to celebrate the most famous TV puppets of the past thirty years, sir?"

"The most FAMOUS?" howled Dad. "The MOST famous?"

"Dad . . . ," I said, dragging on his arm. I was shrugged off quickly.

"It's quite good, isn't it?" said the sales assistant. "We're quite proud of it actually. It took us hours after work—a whole bunch of us—to arrange all the characters just so, so they looked natural and like they were having a really good time. It's great, isn't it?"

"Great? Great?" Dad was spitting. "It's evil! It's an insult!"

The sales assistant seemed a bit disappointed by this. "Oh. We were pleased with it. It brought back all sorts of lovely memories of the puppet TV shows of our childhoods. . . . It was very nostalgic. . . ."

"Pah!" Dad shouted in his face. "Oh, yes, you've got that rubbishy poodle Wilberforce and Danny the bloody bear and Nixon the penguin . . . but where's Tolstoy, eh? Where's my long-eared bat? You've not brought Tolstoy back on video, have you? I'd have known! I'd be raking the cash in by now! Instead . . . you've brought back all these rotten, rubbishy puppets! Puppets no one wants to see again!"

Dad was really going for it now.

"Second-raters! No hopers! None of that lot was a patch on Tolstoy the long-eared bat! Where's he, eh? Why isn't he out there in your so-called lovely display?"

The sales assistant blinked slowly, keeping a tight hold on his stack of merchandise as Dad gesticulated wildly in the aisle. We've got a right one here, he must have been thinking. Oh, we've got a loony here, obsessed with long-eared bats. Keep calm. Don't aggravate him further.

"Er, no, sir . . . ," said the sales assistant cautiously. "No, we haven't. Erm . . . who exactly was Tolstoy the long-eared bat? Was he on the telly as well, sir?"

For a second I thought my old dad was having a violent

heart attack. He went, "Gaagghhh!" as if all of his internal organs were exploding, one after another.

"Of course he was on the telly, you stupid young fool!" Dad said in a suddenly low and calm tone of voice. Only I knew that this calmness was the most dangerous sign of all. "And Tolstoy was a much, much more famous star than any of those . . . useless rags in your precious window!"

With that Dad went stomping off towards the window itself, roughly pushing aside unwary Megastore customers who wandered into his path.

"Don't, Dad!" I cried, knowing instinctively what was going to happen next. I started hurrying after him, but I was way behind. It was like trying to run in some awful dream.

Dad had already clambered into the main window of the Megastore's display.

I tried to catch up, but the sales assistant grabbed me and asked, "Is that mad old coot your grandad? What does he think he's doing? He'll set the alarms off or something! He's mental!"

I yelled back, "He's my dad!" I was suddenly aware of the crowd that was gathering to watch what Dad was up to. And I felt suddenly protective of him. "He's not mental, all right?"

For a second the sales assistant looked abashed.

"He's just a neglected artist," I said. "He gets a bit worked up sometimes, that's all."

Then I took the opportunity to dash away, up to the back of the window display, from which the most terrible noises of mass destruction and calamity were coming. These crashes and roars were drowning out even the thudding dance music in the shop.

"Dad!" I shouted, appalled at what I suddenly saw he was doing. "You can't do that!"

I was on tiptoes, craning my neck over the hardboard back of the display. I saw—with utter horror—that a crowd had gathered on the pavement outside the shop. All of them were mocking and laughing and pointing at the havoc my dad was wreaking.

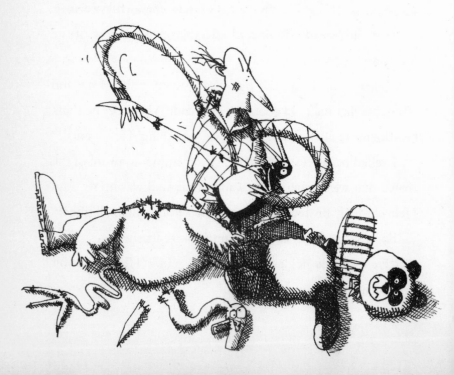

He was right in the middle of the Winter Wonderland. He had fallen on the heap of waving, grinning puppets and he was wrestling with them like a mad thing, like they had all come to demonic life and attacked him first.

He had already wrenched down the sign that read REMEMBER US? in bright, glittering, inviting colors.

Now he was ripping the heads off the ostrich and a panda, picking up a penguin and tearing both wings off, and then shredding the clothes and fur from the lifeless body of a startled-looking fox.

Among the tinsel and polystyrene snow there now lay strewn bits of puppet arms and legs, ears, heads, noses and whiskers. There was stuffing and shreds of plush fur flying about everywhere.

Dad had laid into them all like a whirling dervish and exacted a terrible revenge on these puppets.

"Oh, Dad," I sighed as I took in the extent of his attack. I'd had no idea he was quite this bananas.

"I've killed them!" Dad thundered, completely oblivious of the shocked stares of shoppers on either side of the window. "I've killed them all! And it serves them right! They had it coming to them! Waving and smiling like that! They didn't deserve to live . . . because they forgot about Tolstoy!

How dare they forget the long-eared bat? How dare they forget the two of us?"

Dad gave a great despairing cackle and then, very loudly, began hawking up phlegm and then spitting all over the TV puppets of the past in the window display. Or what was left of them anyway. Soon they were covered in huge gobs of greenish gunk.

"Oh, Dad . . . ," I said again, just as the Megastore's security guards came running up at last with determined looks on their faces. The air was crackling with the noise from their walkie-talkies. "You've really gone too far this time. . . ."

Four

Things happened very quickly after that.

I was forced to step back as the law took its own course. The Megastore's security guards were brave enough to step into the Winter Wonderland, but they decided they had to ring the police to get them to take Dad away.

Meanwhile, Dad had gone into some kind of trance, standing stock still in the midst of the carnage he had created. He was rocking on his heels and mumbling under his breath.

The crowd was still there watching him, though they didn't find it so funny now. They waited until a police car came screaming to a halt outside the shop and you could see that they were excited in a ghoulish kind of a way: watching this dazed old man being taken into custody.

The shop assistant looked at me, concerned. No one else had even realized that the madman being dragged away was my dad. "Are you okay?" he asked.

"Of course I'm not!"

"Look, do you want to go with them? I'm sure they'll let you."

I nodded dumbly and the shop assistant started leading me outside, through the chattering crowd and towards the police car. I could just see Dad being bundled into the back. Suddenly he looked very old and pathetic.

"Here!" the shop assistant shouted. "This is his son here! He wants to go with . . ."

But the burly policemen had clambered into their car, set their siren off again and, before we knew it, the car had roared away at top speed down High Street.

"Oh," said the shop assistant. "They were quite keen, weren't they?"

The crowd around us were gabbling among themselves now, cooing and muttering about all the palaver. The newer members of the audience were being told the story by those who'd witnessed the whole thing: Some daft old man had slaughtered all the puppets in the window display.

In the window itself, the distraught-looking Megastore manager was taking Polaroid snapshots of the puppets. "He's doing that for the insurance," sighed the shop assistant as the bulbs went off brightly.

"I'll have to get home," I said urgently. "I'll have to tell Mam about this."

"Are you sure you're okay?" asked the shop assistant.

"No! I've already said I'm not!"

"Is your dad always like this?"

"Yes! He's crackers!" I said. "But he's never done any-thing as mad as this!"

I took the same bus back home, through the snow. It had been the weirdest shopping trip of my life.

That same woman from our street, the one with the tar-tan shopping bag, got on again. She was loaded down with all kinds of parcels, huffing and puffing.

"Did you leave your old dad behind, eh?" She grinned at me, plonking herself down.

"He's been arrested," I said glumly. "For assaulting some puppets."

"Really?" She beamed. "Isn't that lovely?"

Then she turned to start flirting with the bus conductor, who'd just shoved his ticket machine in her face.

So she was crackers as well.

"Mam!" I found myself yelling in the hallway of our house. I was pulling my wellies off and shouting at the top of my voice. I sounded very young and high-pitched suddenly, even to myself. "Mam! The police came and took Dad away! Mam!"

I yanked my boots off eventually and laid them quickly on

the newspaper in the kitchen. Even in an emergency it didn't do to leave your mucky wellies lying about. We have very particular rules in our house.

"Mam!"

She wasn't listening. I could hear the noise of the telly on full blast in the living room. She'd be in there. She always watched the telly when Dad was out of the house. It was her favorite time.

I burst through the door into the room. She was standing in the middle of the rug, facing the telly, and she had a painting easel out. She was dabbing a brush thoughtfully into the middle of a kind of haphazard landscape, putting some blobby final touches on a messy-looking tree. On the telly, a man with bushy hair was showing her how it ought to be done.

"Oh, Jason!" she gasped, startled, waggling her brush and oil palette in the air. "Is your dad back?" She looked panicked. Those fairy wings she was wearing were quivering at her back.

"No," I said. "It's all right."

She was trying to cover up her painting.

"It's not very good, is it?" she said sadly, surveying it. "It never comes out anything like that bloke's on there." She sighed. "It's the same with the DIY and the gardening. And the cookery. I can't do anything that they do on daytime TV. I'm a complete and utter failure, Jason."

Now Mam was in despair as well! I couldn't believe it!

I hurried over and snapped off the telly.

"Mam!" I said. "This is important!"

She shrugged wretchedly. "So is this! I'm just hoping that one day I can do something right. One day I want to do something just like they do on TV. It could be anything . . . rag-roll a wall, paint some plant pots, bake a perfect soufflé. But, no. I'm useless."

We didn't have time for this. I hated butting in, but I had to.

"Dad's been arrested, Mam! The police came and took him away!"

Suddenly she was out of her sunken gloom. "What?"

"He's at the police station or somewhere! They've locked him up in a cell!"

Mam looked shocked. She also looked as if she didn't know whether to laugh or cry. "Oh! At least he's not found me watching the telly again! He hates that! At least he didn't find me out!"

She was getting hysterical, slapping oil paint about the place.

"Do you think they'll keep him in forever?" she said. "Do you think they'll throw away the key?"

"It's serious, Mam," I said. And I told her what he'd done. Mam went white.

I even told her the bit about when he started gagging up phlegm and spitting over the bits of dead puppets.

Mam sat down quickly on the settee. With her wings on, that paintbrush of hers looked like a funny kind of wand. But she was a useless fairy too and she couldn't magic any of this away.

"I knew he'd do something like this one day," she moaned, rocking herself. "Oh, Frank, you old fool. Why can't you let it go? Why can't you see that you've had your fame and no one cares anymore? Why get angry at a whole load of furry puppets?"

"But what are we going to do?" I asked.

She looked at me. "I don't know. What does one usually do in these circumstances?"

She was talking weirdly to me. I decided that it had probably all been too much for her. She didn't know how to react at all. In a way, she looked glad that Dad was out of her hair for a while.

"I don't know what to do!" I shouted. "I'm only thirteen!"

"Maybe they'll put him on trial," she sighed. "Then he'll be on the telly and in the papers. He'll be happy then." She was struck by another thought. "I'll have to buy a new hat! A whole new outfit."

"Maybe we can get him out on bail," I said thoughtfully. "That's what they do, isn't it?"

"What?" she gasped. "Pay money to get him back?" She looked at me like I was the daft one.

"We have to do *something*, Mam. We can't just leave him in there. . . ."

For a second Mam seemed as if she was toying with the idea. "I suppose you're right." She got up heavily and walked out of the room. "I'll give the police station a ring. I'll say he's not been himself recently."

I nodded.

Then Mam was struck by another thought. "I'm not very good on the phone. Talking with official people and all that. It was your dad who always did that. Will you do it, Jason?"

"Me?"

And so I found myself dialing the police station as Mam read the number out of the phone book. We got through to a kennel at first—wrong number—and they were alarmed to hear I thought they had my dad locked in a cell. Eventually I got to talk with the desk sergeant at the station in town.

"Yes, we've got him. And a nasty piece of work he is too."

"Is he all right?"

"Him? He's as fit as a fiddle, the old devil. He punched one of my men in the nose. He's been shouting fit to burst. He's been yelling for his lawyer."

"Can he come home?"

"No."

"Oh. When can he come home? It's just . . ." I looked at Mam, who was trying to listen in over my shoulder. "It's just my mam's asking."

"No, I'm not," she suddenly hissed. "Tell them they can keep him!"

"He can't come home yet, sonny." The desk sergeant chuckled. "Due procedures have to be gone through. Attacking other people's puppets in a public place . . . well, that's a very serious matter, is that. Oh, no. I think we may well have to throw the whole book at him."

"Really?" I gasped.

"Resisting arrest too," said the desk sergeant. "Do you know he bit one of my lads' ears? We've had to send poor Jenkins for a tetanus. Up to the infirmary."

I commiserated, though I didn't know what a tetanus was. I hissed to Mam, "He's bitten someone on the ear, the policeman says."

"Typical!" she snapped.

"Look, sonny," said the desk sergeant, "why don't we keep him in the cells for a night, hmm? Let him cool down a bit. And then tomorrow you and your mother can come and visit him and we'll know by then what we're charging him with. It could be anything. We're not very sure what the law says with regards to glove puppets. But we've got our very best men looking into it. Good-bye!"

And then the phone went dead.

Mam was looking at me expectantly. "Well, Jason? What's happening?"

"We both have to go down there tomorrow."

"To the police station!" she said, horrified.

"And they don't know what he's guilty of. Whether it's murder or what."

"Murder? How can it be murder? They were only puppets. . . . How can you murder a puppet?"

How indeed?

We were about to find out exactly how many ways there were to murder a puppet. But that was later.

In the meantime Mam was feeling sick with nerves.

"I can't go to the police station! I'm allergic to them! They're worse than hospitals! They'll lock me up as well! I'll never get out!"

"You haven't done anything," I said. "Of course they won't. It's Dad who's in the mess."

She rounded on me bitterly. "Yes, and it's me who has to sort the old fool out. As usual! Well, this isn't like arguing with the window-cleaner or insulting the salesgirl in the shoe shop! This is a serious crime he's committed!"

"I know," I said. "I was there."

"Well, we need help with this," she said.

She was thinking hard, pacing up and down the hallway. Her fairy wings looked ridiculous, bobbing about.

Then she whirled around and said, "I know! I know who'll help us!"

She raced to the address book that she kept on the telephone table. One of those ones where you dial the name in and the pages flip open.

"Who, Mam? Who can help us?"

She produced the right page triumphantly. "I know they hate each other, or they pretend to . . . and I know your dad swore he'd never talk to him again for betraying him . . . but needs must when the devil drives . . ."

She was already dialing the number.

I couldn't believe it. "You don't mean . . ."

"I do!" she said. "I'm calling your half-brother. The arch betrayer!"

"You can't. Dad will go mad. . . ."

"He already *is* mad, Jason."

"But, Mam . . ."

"Shh. It's ringing." Then she put on her poshest voice. "Could I speak to Barry, please?"

Five

It must have been hard for Mam to talk to Barry. He was the son Dad had with his first wife, years before Mam was on the scene. Barry is a few years older than Mam is and she's his stepmother. That's just weird, really, when you think about it. But because Dad won't have anything to do with his first, oldest, successful son, Mam never usually gets to see him.

She was on the phone that night for quite a while. She sat at the bottom of our stairs with the receiver cradled in both hands. I was watching and listening round the front-room door. She looked small, like a young girl, and she was whispering, getting upset, trying to keep a grip on things.

Barry must have been giving her a hard time. She was telling him what had happened to Dad and she was virtually begging him for help.

"I'm not a very practical person, Barry," she hissed into the phone, as if she didn't want me to overhear. "I won't be able to speak up in court and to the police or anything . . . I'll just go to pieces! But you . . . you're a man of the world, Barry. You'll know just the right things to do and to say to get your dad set free. I know the two of you have had your problems in the past. . . ."

She listened then, frowning. Barry must have been ranting down the other end.

"He's still your old dad, Barry," my mam broke in sharply. "That should count for something, whatever he's like . . ."

And so the conversation went on for ages. In the end, though, it seemed that Mam managed to get him to agree. When she put the phone down, I crept back into the hall and she looked at me, more worried than ever.

"He's coming here tomorrow morning," Mam said. She glanced about vaguely, as if checking the house was tidy enough for such elevated company.

"He's going to help us?" For a second I was relieved that someone else was going to take charge.

Mam nodded. "Yes, but . . . on one condition."

"What condition?"

She gave a despairing sigh. One that turned into a stifled sob. "I daren't tell you." Mam looked aghast at what she'd agreed to. "Your dad is going to kill me when he finds out. . . ."

I've never really seen much of Barry. There was one time, about two years ago, at my nan's funeral. Barry turned up in this long silver Rolls-Royce and he had all these people with him that he said were his staff. He had two secretaries, four publicity people, a hairstylist and even someone to hold a black umbrella over him as he walked through the graveyard in the rain.

Even when we were all standing round Nan's grave, Barry and Dad didn't speak to each other.

"I think it's awful," Mam muttered. "Having a rift in the family."

Dad growled, low in his withered throat. "Look at him! Wearing sunglasses in the rain! At his own grandmother's funeral!"

Barry and his entourage didn't stick around long after the do. I was busy thinking about my nan and how I'd miss her. I was thinking how weird it was we'd watched people sticking her in a black hole in the muddy ground. I really loved my nan. She was Dad's mam and she'd been nothing like him. Plump where he was bony; funny where he was plain nasty. She'd been quite a famous exotic dancer in her time. She'd kept on stripping till she was sixty-five and most of the people at her funeral were from the world of entertainment. Not even many of them recognized my dad, which infuriated him even more than usual.

They all recognized Barry, though. Even with his shades on. The old strippers and magicians' assistants whispered and mumbled among themselves at the wake after the funeral. "That's Barry Lurcher . . . the puppeteer! The famous one! Him off the telly! Off Cable TV! That's him, look!"

Barry seemed to drink up all their attention, but he didn't respond to it. Dad bridled and kept his distance. Then Barry was going. Ripples went through the crowded room, where the guests were juggling plates of sandwiches and tiny glasses of sherry. Unexpectedly he came over to me in the hallway of Nan's old house.

"Hey," he said in his famous voice, which always sounded a bit American. "You're my brother, aren't you? Julian, isn't it?"

"Jason," I said, not really minding if he got it wrong. This was someone off the telly. He had a suntanned fleshy face and curly blond hair. He lifted up his shades to show twinkling green eyes. It hit me for the first time that I was actually related to someone really famous.

"Hey," Barry said, "how's the old man? Still nasty and mad? Still bitter and crazy?"

I stared back up at him and nodded. "Yes," I said. "He is. Very."

Barry nodded in satisfaction. "Hey, well, don't tell him I was asking after him. And you look after yourself, okay,

Julian? If you ever need anything, just you let me know. We're brothers, right?"

I nodded dumbly and then I watched Barry turn, gather up his retinue of paid helpers and walk out of Nan's house and my life. That was two years ago. None of us had seen him since. Only on the telly. Only on *The Barry Lurcher Show* on Cable TV.

Me and Mam were forbidden to watch that. But sometimes, secretly, we did.

* * *

I went to bed quite late that night.

My head was still racing with the day's hectic events. Some of them had been horrible. All of them had been bizarre.

Our house felt quite different without Dad in it. Quieter. There wasn't that awful, pervading, malignant atmosphere of imminent doom. There was a whole lot of fretting in the air instead. Mam kissed me good night distractedly. She was drifting about the place in a flowery housecoat, sipping Baileys out of a mug and saying it was cold hot chocolate.

I went to bed in my small room at the top of the house. It had been mine for all of my life. I didn't have much stuff in it.

I slept for a little while and had these very confusing dreams about sitting on the bus with Dad, sliding through the banked-up snow on the way into town. Then I could see him in the Megastore's window, attacking and ripping up all of the glove puppets again. Laughter and gasps and Dad's cries of rage. I was shouting out, telling him to stop, all over again. Sirens were shrieking, sirens wailing . . . I think I was shouting out in my sleep, deep in the thickest part of the night.

I shouted myself awake. I sat bolt upright in my lumpy, narrow bed. My heart was hammering hard.

Every moment of my dreams had been true. All of those things had really happened that day.

The moon was full and milky and it shone clearly through my bedroom window. There weren't any curtains.

I couldn't believe I'd been shouting out in my sleep.

What was worse, something was shouting back.

It wasn't Mam.

The voice was coming from above. Through the ceiling of my room.

A vile, rasping, ghostly voice.

I sat up in bed and clutched my knees. I bundled my duvet up and craned my ears.

There was only the attic up there. There was nothing in our attic. Just old junk. Nobody could be up there, calling through the dusty floorboards . . . calling out to me . . .

I listened.

It came again.

"Destiny, is it?" the voice was saying. "Is that what the old fart's been telling you? That nasty shriveled-up old devil? Well, it's true. I am your destiny. You're my new master. You have to come here, young Jason. One day soon you'll come up to the attic. You'll open up the old trunk. You'll know what you're looking for. You're looking for me. . . . And I'm up here waiting. . . ."

Then that horrible raspy voice dissolved into evil laughter.

Then silence.

I lay back, stunned.

And drifted back into sleep again.

Six

When I came down for breakfast the next morning my head was thick with all kinds of foreboding. And it wasn't just because Mam was on this health lark and we had to eat all kinds of muck that she'd invented, like her own muesli, which resembled something off the bottom of a budgie's cage. No, there were other reasons why I felt nervous.

I was halfway down the stairs when a piercing shriek came from the hallway. Mam had opened the front door to someone and she was screaming at the top of her voice. It was half-past eight in the morning. Surely Barry couldn't have turned up so soon? And if he had, why was she yelling at him? She'd asked him to come to our house in the first place. I thudded down the rest of the stairs.

There was a whole load of people outside our house, jostling at the front door. Mam was still screaming in her flowery housecoat and slippers, her hair all over the place from sleeping on it.

"What is it, Mam?"

She looked at me with her eyes wide. Her hands flew up to arrange her bird's-nest hair. "Go and get some clothes on," she hissed. "Get out of those pajamas and put something smart on, our Jason!"

The people crowding through our front door were carrying all sorts of strange objects. Tripods and cables and heavy metal lamps. They came traipsing into our house, past Mam and me, as if they owned the place. It was only when two burly men lugging sophisticated-looking cameras came in that I started to realize what was going on.

"Are we going to be on the telly, Mam?"

Her hands were covering up her mouth like she couldn't

trust herself to answer. I think she had gone into shock.

"Hey, Eileen! Julian!" boomed a deep and hearty voice. Its accent was almost American. It was the happiest-sounding voice there'd been in our house for years. But it was a false kind of happy. You could tell that it was just put on.

My brother, Barry, was striding into our house with his horde of hangers-on.

He was in a very expensive-looking blue suit and his curly hair was gleaming with hairspray. He had his usual secretaries and publicists with him, and also another camera trained on him as he grinned at us two in our night things. Then he turned to gaze around at our front hallway.

Out of the corner of his mouth he hissed at the skinny cameraman, "Make sure you're focused right in on me. Get all of my reactions. This is a big moment. This is the horrible house I grew up in, remember. It's a very poignant moment, this."

The skinny cameraman crouched down below Barry and fiddled anxiously with his equipment, trying his best to get the angle right.

When things seemed to be to Barry's satisfaction, he turned to Mam and me with a droopy, woeful expression and his arms wide open. He smothered us with a huge cuddle. He reeked of some spicy aftershave, very expensive no doubt.

"Hey, my poor stepmother, Eileen! And my poor, poor neglected half-brother, Julian! Let me comfort you both in your hour of dire need."

So we had to stand there for a bit, surrounded by all these technical people, as Barry hugged us. Mam was certainly in shock and I think I was too, by now. Barry was a bit fatter than the last time we'd seen him.

"Mam," I whispered, "why's he going on like this? And why are they filming us?"

She looked at me tearfully. "They're making a documentary." She seemed very ashamed as Barry crushed her face into his ample chest. "That was the bargain. He'd help us if his production company could make a documentary about it. To show what a caring human being he is."

"Ssssh," Barry growled at her, and then he set us free. He looked at us both seriously. "Hey, so tell me what's happening. What are they doing with . . ." He gave a choked kind of sob. Completely fake. "What are they doing to my dad?"

Mam opened her mouth to reply.

"Okay, cut!" shouted Barry. "We'll cut it there and then we'll pick up with an interview in the living room. Five minutes long, I think. A proper in-depth interview." He rubbed his palms together and grinned at us again. "The viewers are going to love this. Hey, this is great. Full of pathos. We might even win an award. . . ."

Mam's face had gone black with anger. "Barry, when I said you could film this and make a documentary, I didn't mean . . ."

"Hey, Eileen." He smiled. "Calm down, lady."

"I didn't mean you could film me in my housecoat and nightie! Look at me! I look a complete fright!"

On cue, three make-up girls appeared as if by magic and started fiddling with Mam's hair and slapping her about with a pink powder puff. Mam snarled and shooed them away. It was true, though. She did look a fright.

"Hey, Eileen." Barry shrugged. "The TV audience loves all that. It's like real life. It's verisimilitude. They love seeing people looking terrible, with their hair all messy and their eyes all blotchy from crying. Hey, it's great TV!"

Mam was livid. "I don't care! If I have to be on telly, I WANT TO LOOK FANTASTIC!"

Barry was ignoring her. He was rummaging around in a sports bag. He nodded to his skinny cameraman and I realized we were going to be filmed again.

"Never mind, stepmother Eileen!" he cried in his cheerful voice. "Look who's here to help you in your time of greatest need!"

"What?" spluttered Mam. "What are you talking about?"

Barry grinned the whitest, most dazzling grin I'd ever seen. "Hey . . . why, look who it is!"

Then he yanked a life-sized furry penguin out of the bag. It sat on his free arm and flapped its stumpy wings. Its glass eyes seemed to be glinting with sympathy as it looked at us.

"Hey, it's Nixon the penguin, everybody," said Barry consolingly. "And he's here to put a smile back on all your faces!"

Mam and I both stared back dumbly at the goggle-eyed Nixon.

"Cut!" cried Barry.

"I don't want to be interviewed by a bloody penguin!" Mam was shouting. I could hear her even though I was back up in my room, hurriedly dressing.

Everything had been a bit weird this morning, but I was

quite excited. It wasn't every day we had a complete TV crew in our house.

"Look, Barry," I could hear Mam yelling, "we've got to go to that police station and get your poor dad out of the cells! There isn't any time to mess around talking to bleeding puppets!"

At least Mam had got some of her spirit back. I hadn't heard her so worked up in years.

Actually, I was quite pleased to have met the actual, real Nixon the penguin. He was a lot smaller, though, than he seemed on the telly.

I was just about to rush back downstairs to be supportive for Mam when a voice started talking to me from above.

A nasty, scratchy voice that I'd heard in the middle of last night.

I had hoped it was part of my dream.

"I can smell penguin!" rasped the voice. "That rotten penguin's in the house, isn't he? Someone's brought another puppet into this house!"

I looked up at the ceiling of my room. I licked my lips and asked aloud, "Who . . . W-who are you?"

The voice gave an oily chuckle. "Like I said, Jason, I am your destiny. You will be my new master."

"B-but . . ."

"Silence! And I'm telling you, Jason Lurcher, there'll be no more puppets brought into this house. No more puppets but me!"

"Are you—" But I was interrupted again.

"The penguin must go!" wailed the voice from above. "Nixon the penguin must die!"

I really thought I was going crackers.

I put on my trainers and hurtled downstairs.

Madness was in the family. Just look at my dad recently. And Barry couldn't be right in the head. Mam always said my old nan was barmy for going on stripping till she was sixty-five. Now I was hearing voices coming out of the attic.

I must have completely lost it!

All the TV crew were in our living room. They'd set their lights and cameras up by now and everyone was crouched around the chintz settee. There was almost complete hush.

Mam had changed her outfit in record time and looked like a million dollars. However depressed she was, she could act quickly if it meant looking her best. She was in a purple frock with wide shoulders and a low neckline. Her hair was teased up and rock solid with gel. She was sitting demurely, knee to knee on the settee with Barry, who was wearing his most earnest expression. And on Barry's knee perched Nixon the penguin, his orange flipper-feet stuck out in front of him, turning his smooth head from Mam to Barry as they spoke.

I stood in the doorway quietly, listening in to their interview.

Mam dabbed her eyes with a paper hanky. "No one really knows what it's been like living with Frank . . ."

Both Barry and Nixon gave understanding nods.

"When did all of this puppet-related madness begin?" asked Barry.

"He's always been obsessed," said Mam. "You know that, Barry. It's never gone away, even though he won't talk about his glory days. But . . . once a puppeteer, always a puppeteer. I think it's become too much for him at last."

Her interviewers nodded. Then Nixon asked a question of his own. His voice was slightly higher-pitched than Barry's.

"Is it the first time he's ever been violent towards puppets?" Nixon asked.

I was amazed. You could see Barry's lips moving as the penguin talked! He was a rubbish puppeteer! They must use editing trickery when he was on telly.

Mam looked the penguin straight in the eye. "Yes, I think so. Oh, Frank rants and shouts, but he's never been violent before. I've never seen him actually hit a puppet. Certainly I've never known him to . . . rip them up into pieces!"

She collapsed into tears, clutching her hanky to her face.

The penguin was shuddering in fear.

"Cut! That's a wrap!" Barry called delightedly. "That's enough for the moment, I think, everyone. Now it's time to get to the police station. We can film Dad locked up in his cell!"

Seven

I was the one who'd been there. I'd witnessed the whole thing; what Barry was calling our dad's "descent into puppet-related madness." But no one had asked me a single thing.

Now I was sitting in a big silver van full of TV people and we were speeding through the snowy streets to the police station. Mam was sitting up in the front with Barry and the driver. She was being filmed looking all concerned, staring out at the wintry streets of our town.

"Oh, it's going to be very artistic, this documentary," said the woman sitting beside me. "I bet we win all kinds of awards."

I looked at her. She had these very large, round blue eyes, a snub nose and streaky blonde hair. She was holding three brushes, two big combs and a mammoth can of hairspray. She was Barry's own personal hairstylist and was responsible for making his shaggy permed hair perfect for the cameras. She also groomed all of his furry puppets, including Nixon the penguin.

She held out her hand for me to shake. "I'm Lisa Turmoil," she said breathily. "Hairstylist to the stars." She was wearing a denim jacket and skirt and I wondered how old she was, to have all that responsibility.

I blinked. "I'm Jason."

"I know." She smiled. "This must be a very difficult time for you."

"It is!" I agreed. "Everything's gone completely mad."

"Well," she said, "we're here now, filming everything. You should find that very reassuring. Seeing it all on the telly."

"Why?"

She stared at me. "Because . . . that makes everything seem better, doesn't it? If you see it on the telly."

"Does it?"

"Sure," said Lisa Turmoil. "Things don't really happen until they're on the telly. They don't even *exist* until they're on the telly. Everyone knows that."

"Oh."

We were squashed up together then, as the TV crew's van slewed round an icy corner. I realized that all the make-up women and the technical guys were watching me talk with the hairstylist. I suddenly felt a bit shy.

"You are all going to be very famous," Lisa Turmoil told me.

"I don't want to be famous," I said.

Lisa looked shocked. "But everyone wants to be on *The Barry Lurcher Show*! Everyone wants to meet Nixon the penguin."

"I don't," I said. I sounded a bit huffy. "Barry's a rubbish puppeteer. You can see his lips moving."

Lisa started to laugh and she stopped herself quickly. "Hush! You can't say that, Jason. Nobody's allowed to point that out."

"I bet he isn't a patch on what my dad was like," I said. I was surprised at myself, sticking up for Dad.

Lisa nodded. "I've heard your dad was the greatest of them all."

"Have you?"

She smiled. "Even Barry admits that. Sometimes. If only your dad hadn't fallen out with Tolstoy the long-eared bat . . ." She sighed and juggled her hairbrushes thoughtfully. We careened around another sharp corner. "Fancy having a row with your own glove puppet, live on a TV chat show," she said. "If they hadn't done that, your dad would still be on the telly to this day."

"I know," I said sadly. "And then he wouldn't be crazy and we wouldn't be visiting him in the police cells . . ."

"Oh, he'd still have been crazy," said Lisa. "All puppeteers are bonkers, obviously. Who else would go round talking to their hands and making their hands answer back?" She laughed. She had a laugh like a donkey. It took some getting used to. "Do you know, everyone in this crew has to call that penguin Mr. Nixon? Back at the studios, that rotten glove puppet has got his own dressing room! How mad is that?"

I smiled at her. "That's pretty mad."

"Still," said Lisa, "at least Nixon's got a nicer personality than Barry. Barry can be a monster. Very temperamental, these puppeteers."

I decided I liked Lisa Turmoil, hairstylist to the stars. She talked sense, I thought. And she talked to me like I wasn't just some daft kid.

When the van pulled to an abrupt halt a few moments later, she said, "Come on, then, Jason, love. We're here. Time to visit your poor old dad."

Everyone was collecting up their equipment, ready for the next shoot.

All I could think was: She called me "love"! For a few minutes I found that quite dizzying—and I don't think it was just the fumes from all the hairspray.

The police station was cramped and gloomy. The walls were bare brick painted sickly green. Inside, it smelled of corned-beef toasties, floor cleaner and a faint tang of wee. Our party was jostling for space in the waiting room, surrounded by hideous faces on "Wanted" posters.

The desk sergeant was a huge man, bursting out of the

silver buttons of his uniform. I wondered if he was the one I"d talked to on the phone, and as soon as he opened his mouth I knew he was.

"Nasty piece of work, he is," said the policeman, playing it up for the cameras. "Can't see what you want to make a documentary about him for. You should make one about me. We see all sorts of action round here. And people like watching TV shows about policemen."

Mam was sniffling into her hanky again and I thought she was playing up to the cameras too. Barry was resting Nixon the penguin on the police sergeant's desk. You could see his fat hand sticking up the penguin's bum. Even I knew that was the first thing a good puppeteer kept hidden from sight.

"Can we see him?" asked Nixon in his shrill voice, his beak moving slightly out of time. "Can we go into the cells and interview Barry's dad?"

The cell was very bleak and bare—just one barred window near the ceiling and a tiny little bunk. Dad looked older than ever. About a hundred years old. Unshaven, he seemed wild, like he'd been on the streets for a month. His spartan hair was sticking right up in the air. He looked utterly defeated.

He peered cautiously through the bars of his cell as we

trooped in to see him. He looked confused at the sight of all these people.

"Keep back from the bars," the desk sergeant advised us gruffly. "He's had a go at a few of my men. . . ."

Dad came shuffling forward. It was like visiting him in the zoo.

The camera was trained on my mam as she went to the bars and flung herself against them, wailing loudly. "Oh, Frank, Frank," she cried. "What have they done to you? Have they tortured you, darling? Are they going to send you to prison?"

Dad stared at her. "Eileen?" he frowned. "Why are you shouting? What's the matter with you? And who are all these people?"

Actually, he sounded quite reasonable.

Mam was still going on. "We'll get you out, Frank. We'll do anything to get you set free."

"But . . . ," said Dad dazedly, "they'll let me out today, pending charges. They've already told me—"

Mam wasn't listening. "Have they broken your spirit, my darling? Are you a broken man?"

"Eileen," he said. "I . . ." But then he saw the camera trained beadily on him. And what's more, he saw Barry standing there, all gleaming, professional and grinning.

Dad snarled. For a second he looked exactly like a caged beast. Then he started bellowing all over again. My mad old, bad old dad was back. "What's HE doing here?" he screeched, thrusting a bony finger through the cell bars at his eldest son. "The betrayer! The traitor within! The incubus!"

"Watch out," the policeman said. "He's going loopy again."

"Now, now, Dad," said Barry mildly. "You don't want to be saying nasty things, do you?"

Dad growled. "Why not? You treacherous cur!" He rattled the bars.

"Because, Daddy dearest," Barry simpered, "we're on the telly." He nodded at the camera, which the skinny cameraman was training on the two of them.

They were in close-up.

Dad looked startled. "Why are we on telly?"

"Oh, Frank," sobbed Mam, "I thought it would help. Help us get proper justice. If Barry's company made a tasteful TV docu-drama all about your fight for freedom and justice . . ."

Everyone watched Dad's face as it twitched up in a series of terrifying expressions. It went through rage and horror and torment and fury and panic and hatred and back to plain rage again. I closed my eyes, waiting for the inevitable explosion.

But Dad calmed down. His face went placid and he suddenly looked almost normal. Pleased, even.

Everyone was relieved.

Dad nodded. "Very well. Put me on the telly. Tell my story to the whole world if you like."

Barry beamed. "That's more like it, Dad. We'll make a wonderful show about you. About your awful plight."

Then Barry was holding Nixon the penguin up to the bars. The penguin was leaning in to Dad's face and saying in his squeaky voice, "You know it makes sense, Frank!"

Dad's eyes blazed viciously.

And before anyone knew it and before anyone could leap in to stop him, Dad's gnarled old hands shot right through the bars.

They seized the startled penguin round the neck.

"Don't talk to me, you puppet!" Dad shrieked.

"Ow! Owww!" howled Barry.

The rest of us were frozen, appalled, where we stood.

"Die, Nixon! Die, puppet!" Dad screamed.

And, relishing every malicious second of it, he started to throttle the penguin.

Eight

Who'd have thought that Lisa Turmoil, hairstylist to the stars, could have moved so fast?

All the rest of us could do was hang back in shocked silence as Dad grimly continued to strangle Nixon. The penguin was squawking and flapping his wings and Barry was yelping in pain as his fingers were crushed.

It was Lisa Turmoil who darted forward with her heaviest hairbrushes and brought them down hard on both of Dad's hands. She cracked them down with a crunch and a thwack on his bony knuckles and he was stunned into letting go of his victim.

Then he screamed out in pain.

Barry fell back, hugging his penguin co-star to his chest.

Dad nursed his wounded hands and bellowed at us all, "I'll not be spoken to by puppets! Never again, do you hear me?"

The desk sergeant shook his head, tutting. "See what I mean? What a vicious old man he is. I reckon we'll need to put him in a straitjacket for you to take him home."

Lisa was juggling her hairbrushes like a gunslinger, clearly pleased with her handy intervention. I was amazed at her speed, but I was also a bit upset. She'd hurt my dad, after all.

Barry, meanwhile, stroked his penguin's head, muttering, "There, there . . ."

"He nearly killed me!" Nixon gibbered. "I was almost a goner there."

The policeman came back with a dirty-looking garment, all buckles and straps, with these extra long arms that would tie up at the back. It was so Dad wouldn't be able to attack anyone else.

Mam looked mortified at the sight of the straitjacket. "Oh, Frank," she said. She looked at the cameraman. "Can you stop filming this bit? Is nothing private?"

Dad gave a harsh, cruel laugh. "Not exactly high fashion, is it, Eileen? What's the matter? Ashamed of being seen out in public with me if I'm all strapped up?"

Mam was hurt by this. "How can you say that, Frank? I'm standing by you, through the shame of this whole nightmare. . . ."

"Oh, yes?" he said. "And that includes bringing my hated first son in to see me, does it?"

"I thought he could help, Frank," Mam wailed.

Dad's eyes still blazed that weird, unearthly green. "He doesn't want to help me. He'd rather see me dead. His own dad, dead!"

* * *

They released Dad into our custody and he was led out to Barry's silver van, all dressed up in the dirty buckled strait-jacket. As we settled down for the short ride back to our house, he seemed a bit more resigned and subdued.

"They've sedated him," Lisa Turmoil whispered to me, as we sat back in our seats.

We all looked at Dad, slumped and trussed by himself at the back of the van. He was muttering now, as the van started moving. He was going, "Puppets, puppets, puppets, puppets," under his rank breath.

"It's all right, Frank," Mam called worriedly from the front passenger seat. "We'll have you home soon. I'll make your favorite dinner. You can relax and calm down. . . ."

Barry, pointedly, didn't say anything to Dad. Nixon the penguin had been stowed away, back in his sports bag, for safety's sake.

They were going to drop us off at our house and call an end to the day's filming.

"We've got loads of great stuff," said the cameraman, looking very pleased. "A good day's work."

The TV company–people were all going to a swanky hotel in the middle of town. Barry had a suite of rooms at the top, he said. He was going to conduct an extra interview with Nixon, as the penguin struggled to overcome the physical and psychological impact of Dad's nasty assault on him.

"See?" Lisa Turmoil whispered to me, as we drove home. "Crackers. All puppeteers are."

But that worried me even more. I had the same genes in me, didn't I?

Dad had said it was my destiny too to become a puppeteer.

Was I going to be crackers as well?

I didn't want to think about it.

"Don't worry," Lisa said. She patted my knee and smiled.

I was starting to like the smell of hairspray.

Once we got home and the cameramen shot a few pictures of us leading Dad carefully back through the front door, they left us alone at last. Mam and me were on our own with Dad.

He just stood there, trussed up, looking half asleep.

Mam put on this show of being extra cheery, as if nothing weird had happened.

"Well! Shall I put the kettle on? What do you want for dinner, Frank? Jason? Shall I do your favorite, Frank? I've got a packet of Vesta Chow Mein in the cupboard. We could have soft noodles and crispy noodles and . . ."

Dad's voice came out all weak and tired.

"Um . . . could you untie me please, Eileen?"

Mam looked at me. Then she looked at Dad. Her hands fluttered helplessly.

"Do you think that's a good idea?"

"I can't stay wrapped up like this forever, can I?"

Mam was dithering in our hallway. "You . . . you aren't going to hurt either of us, are you, Frank?"

Dad looked appalled. "Of course not, you silly woman! Why would I ever hurt either of you two?"

"You hurt Barry," she said. "You tried to throttle his penguin friend. You would have succeeded too, if that hairdresser hadn't hit you with her brushes."

Dad scowled. "That was because he talked to me through his puppet. I couldn't help myself."

Mam still looked agitated.

"Look," Dad said, "untie me. I'm not going to go funny again. For one thing, I'm too tired. But there's no danger here anyway, is there? There aren't any puppets here, are there?"

There was a pause as Mam weighed up the options. She hated seeing Dad in the straitjacket, I could tell. And it wasn't just a fashion thing.

I knew how soft-hearted Mam was and she still felt something for the old man, after everything. She was convinced he'd be safe out of the jacket. She knew there were no dangerous puppets about the place.

Though I knew different.

Mam started to set him free.

Dad trogged off for a lie down and Mam went to make a pot of tea and set about preparing his favorite meal. She'd feel better with something practical to do, to take her mind off all the recent, terrible events.

She sent me up to my own room, saying I could do with a rest too. I think it was just to get me out of the way, really. As it was, I had a plan of my own. Something I wanted to do anyway. Something secret.

I went upstairs as quietly as I could. Mam was clattering away in the kitchen below. She'd turned on Radio 2 quite loudly, drowning out the sound of her own thoughts. She was singing along in a shrill voice to some old song by Abba. "Super Trouper."

I crept past my parents' bedroom. The door was open and the curtains were drawn. The weak winter sun came filtering through orange. Dad was lying on top of the duvet with his beaky nose thrust up in the air. I thought I could get past without him noticing, but he looked up as I crossed the hall.

"Jason?"

I froze. "Yes, Dad?"

After everything, I was a bit scared of him and it showed in my voice.

"Jason," he said again. "You're the good son. You won't betray your old dad, will you?" He was looking straight at me.

"N-no, Dad."

He smiled. A ghastly sight. "I'm sorry, son," he said. "For all of this palaver. You've seen things you should never have to. Not a kid your age. But you must understand that . . . it's just that . . . when I see puppets . . . I go a little crazy sometimes. . . ."

"I know, Dad."

"So I'm sorry that you've been with me when I've

flipped out . . . and attacked some glove puppets. I'm really sorry for that."

"It's okay."

"I still love you, son," he said, all choked up. "I'm still your dad, you know."

We stood quietly for a second. I was in the doorway, absorbing what he'd said.

"One more thing," he went on. "Tell your mam . . ."

I nodded. "That you love her too?"

"What? Well, yes, I suppose so. No, but if she does do Vesta Chow Mein for dinner, mind she doesn't burn the crispy noodles in the frying pan. I can't stick those burned ones."

"All right, Dad," I said, and closed the bedroom door on him.

I went straight up to the attic.

There was something I had to check. You might think me mad for this. It was a completely daft thing to do. But I had to know. I'd had the question burning inside of me, all day, ever since the middle of last night.

This was my first chance to check it out.

The entrance to our attic was in a cupboard across the hall from my bedroom. It was up a metal ladder and through a dusty hatchway. I hoped I could make it—creaking on every aluminium step—without Mam or Dad hearing me. They'd want to know what I was up to and there was no way I could tell them.

If I told them, they'd think I was deliberately trying to send Dad crackers again. That's how they would see it. But nothing could be further from the truth.

Creak, creak, clang, creak, clang, creak creak, clang . . . I stole up the metal ladder as quickly as I could. Breathing in the scent of dust and the trapped sunlight from the wide attic space.

The room at the top was bigger than I'd thought, and it was filled with radiant orange light. The top of the house caught the last of the December sun's rays. The water tank was burbling softly behind the heaps of boxes and amassed, abandoned junk. I found that the sloping roof of the house left enough room for me to stand up straight in the attic space.

I balanced on the wooden struts, careful not to step on the fluffy pink loft insulation, knowing it was only plaster underneath and wouldn't hold my weight.

I started picking though junk. Broken lampshades, photo albums, gramophone records, chairs, dolls, bags of old clothes. I knew what I was looking for.

It didn't take long.

It was as if that old, battered blue trunk was wanting to

be found. It was under a cardboard box of ancient copies of the *Radio Times* with yellowed pages and frayed corners.

The trunk was fastened securely with leather straps and on its side was stencilled PROPERTY OF FRANK LURCHER. HANDLE WITH EXTREME CARE.

"Care" was crossed out, and someone had replaced it with "Caution," in felt tip.

I gulped. I couldn't believe I was ransacking through Dad's things. Stuff he'd put away, like his old life, never to be opened up again. But here I was. This had to be done. I had to know.

I knelt down and started to unbuckle all the leather straps keeping the trunk shut. My fingers shook slightly and I had to stop for a moment to quell my nerves.

I thought I heard a noise.

Someone coming up the ladder? Were they going to catch me?

No. There was no one coming up.

I was safe.

Then, the final strap fell away.

I was ready to open the trunk.

Nine

He was under there.

He was inside there somewhere.

I knew it as soon as I heaved the heavy lid open and the rusty old hinges squealed in protest.

The trunk was filled to the brim with sawdust and wood shavings, and at first that was all I could see. They were there to protect and cushion the thing that lived inside.

And I knew he was in there.

Waiting.

The sawdust was there to keep him cozy in transit, though he and the trunk hadn't moved from this exact spot in twenty years. For longer than I'd been alive.

I took a deep breath and plunged both my hands into the trunk. The sawdust and shavings tickled and scratched as I groped about, exploring the depths.

It took a moment, but then I found him.

I could feel fur. Tattered, scraggy fur.

I felt the leathery sheen of a wing, the smooth baldness of an extra-large ear.

My pulse thudded busily in my throat. I could hardly breathe.

I had found Tolstoy the long-eared bat.

Very carefully, very slowly, I drew him out of the trunk where he'd been hibernating. His body felt empty and slack in my hands.

I held him up to the meager light of the attic and shook him free of the clinging sawdust and shavings.

His dull glass eyes glared back at me. I was holding him by his large, flapping, velvety ears.

He was the the most hideous thing I had ever seen in all my life.

* * *

It's weird that Tolstoy ever got on the telly in the first place. Even before he had the nasty fight with Dad on that chat show. That was when they fell from grace in the public's eye. They'd screamed insults and swearwords at each other and it had turned very nasty and stopped being funny. Then their show was cancelled. They appeared on a game show or two after that, suffering under a kind of truce, but it was never the same again. Their showbiz partnership was at an end. The old magic had gone. Fled into the night, or wherever old and useless magic flees to.

No, what I mean is that it's surprising to me that anyone ever liked or watched Tolstoy in the first place. He was the vilest-looking, dirtiest, foul-mouthed creature anyone had ever clapped eyes on. Wilberforce the poodle was witty and hilarious; he always had an answer for everything. Charlie the duck was charming and smart. The two singing pigs could perform any song you'd ever heard in their fine and indefatigable falsettos. But Tolstoy the long-eared bat had no discernible talent whatsoever. He'd flap his purple, leathery wings, toss his extra-large ears back in hauteur and pour scorn on everything around him.

He hated Dad, who was meant to be his best friend. He hated the studio audience who came to see his show. He hated the guts of the guests who came to guest-star. He despised the magicians with their leggy assistants and their rubbishy acts where they made doves pop out of tall hats, or pulled silk scarves out of their sleeves. He vilified the singers and dancers who came traipsing out in spangly outfits to waste precious moments of the TV show that bore his name.

They were wasting time that could be filled with more of *him*! Him swearing and ranting and pouring forth the worst invective he could dream up. Tolstoy, of course, told everyone how much he hated them. How much he hoped they realized they were rubbish and they weren't worth his time. He told the Queen to go and boil her head. That was when he met her at the Royal Variety Performance one year at the height of his career. He told her she was a stuck-up old tart and a burden on the state. Her Majesty just laughed toothily, like everyone did, thinking it was a joke. Wasn't the puppet awful? Wasn't he just the funniest, cheekiest thing ever?

And Tolstoy was. He went round flapping his wings and long ears and crossing his skinny black velvety legs and saying the worst things that came into his cankered mind. And, for most of the time, he got away with it. He was a puppet. He had a talent to amuse.

How do I know all of this? I, who was born long after

Tolstoy had been exiled to his trunk, trapped in all the saw-dust, banged up in the attic forever?

Well, I read the newspaper clippings in Dad's old albums. I smuggled them out with me and read them through that night. I caught up on all the stuff that Dad didn't want to tell me, and that Mam didn't dare. I found out, to my amaze-ment, exactly how famous my dad—and his horrible bat—had been back then.

Dad would have killed me if he'd known what I was doing that night. Especially in his fragile, mentally disturbed state. It might have tipped him right over the edge.

I read these albums and articles with the puppet sat on the end of the bed. It was lifeless, of course. But it was staring at me with these green glass eyes that gleamed with a dull, scratched luster.

I turned pages quickly and read by torchlight and Tolstoy sat there.

His fur was matted and filthy.

I really hoped he didn't have fleas.

Another dream.

Vivid, incredible, just like last night's.

Not one of those you can switch off or change, or turn into something nicer.

The dream was too strong. There was no escaping it.

I was in my pajamas and carrying the long-eared bat. Tolstoy was cradled in my arms like a horrible hairy baby with massive ears. It was pitch-black and silent in the night. I was shuffling out of our house, closing the front door behind us. I was outside at night in the snow and in the moonlight.

I started walking. The streets were empty. My head was empty. I had no idea where we were going in this dream. Then the thought hit me: It was all Tolstoy's idea.

The bat had had an idea. And I was being pulled along in its wake.

I had no choice but to follow Tolstoy's lead.

Yet still he lay lifeless in my arms. His purple wings and ears drooping, his velvet legs dangling and swaying as we walked.

We were heading into town. That's the way we went walking. My frozen feet in my slippers slithered and slid on the pavement, the only sound in all these streets.

We were walking into town. I didn't know why.

"Tolstoy?" I asked, but he didn't reply.

The next thing I remember from my dream was that we were standing right in the middle of the town center. It was snowing now and these bright fat flakes were tumbling down around us, catching on my pajamas and in Tolstoy's ragged black fur.

Town was still and only a few lights were burning. Traffic lights, a scattering of Christmas fairy lights and the dim glow of the closed-up shops. Then the brilliance—the welcoming brilliance—of the hotel in front of us. The poshest hotel in all of our town, with its lights ablaze all through the night and potted palms standing outside by its golden front doors.

"What are we doing here, Tolstoy?" I asked the lifeless puppet. "How come you've brought me here?"

I looked away from the dazzling lights of the hotel and then down at the puppet I was holding.

Tolstoy's eyes were burning a livid green.

And then I heard his voice again.

But I don't remember a single thing he said.

I woke up. It's like one of those stories where you get to the exciting bit and then the person in the story tells you it was all just a dream. And that's exactly what this was. I was pleased. I was grateful to wake up in my narrow bed at the top of our house to find that it was the next morning. I was pleased to see that Tolstoy was lying face down on the rug in my room. His eyes hadn't been burning green at all and he hadn't started talking to me. We hadn't walked into town in the snow and the middle of the night.

I got up in a rush and picked up all of the newspaper

clippings and photo albums from Dad's old life as a star puppeteer. I'd pinched them without permission. I had to hide them away in the wardrobe. Mam and Dad couldn't find out what I'd been up to. I bundled everything away out of sight.

I turned to Tolstoy and picked him up gently.

He'd have to be put away too. Hidden in my wardrobe, with all my secret things.

His fur was wet.

His scraggy old fur was damp . . . but how?

It felt just like melted snow, dripping off his arrogant snout and his extra-long and none-too-elegant ears.

I decided I'd think about it later. I shoved him in the wardrobe and wedged the door tight closed. I acted quickly because there was a commotion on the staircase. Mam was shouting for me. She was shouting for Dad too and she was sounding distraught.

What now?

I hurried out. Leaned over the banister.

"That was Barry on the phone!" she was wailing up the staircase. "He was phoning from his suite in the Ritzy Hotel! He's gone mental with grief, he says! He sounds ever so upset!"

I could hear Dad out on his own landing, shouting back

down to Mam. "What are you shouting about, you silly woman?" he said gruffly.

"Oh, it's a tragedy, Frank! You must come down!"

"What?" he said. "What's a tragedy?"

Mam's voice went even higher.

"It's Nixon the penguin! He's been murdered in the middle of the night!"

Ten

Mam decided that we oughtn't to take Dad with us. It was too chancy, what with the state he was in already. After what he'd tried to do to Nixon yesterday, she figured that Barry wouldn't want to see him just now anyway.

She became all calm and sorted out. She sent Dad back to their room and then she called us a taxi to the hotel.

Dad voiced the question that was running through my head. "For God's sake, Eileen. How can anyone murder a glove puppet? It's only a puppet. A thing of stuffing and fabric! It's not like it's a real penguin or anything."

Mam wasn't having any of it. She yelled back up the staircase at Dad. "You never heard your Barry on the phone! He's gone to pieces. He woke up this morning and found poor Nixon lying there, in his own little bed . . . hacked to pieces!"

"His own little bed!" Dad cackled and scoffed. "That penguin had his own little bed!"

Mam's voice went cold. "If you had one shred of natural human feeling in you, Frank Lurcher, then you'd understand what your poor son Barry is going through right now. . . ."

"Pah," said Dad. "I've had my fill of glove puppets. It's a

86

mug's game. You end up just like that daft Barry. Thinking they're real. Getting all upset over them . . ."

"Oh, just go back to bed." Mam dismissed him. "Me and Jason will go to the hotel and see what we can do. Are you ready to go, Jason?"

I was pulling on my wellies. I'd peeked outside. The overnight snow was standing twelve inches deep.

Mam was in a lime-green woolen coat that flared out like a skirt and wore a matching hat the width of a cartwheel. She popped on a pair of sunglasses.

"There's bound to be press attention," she said thoughtfully, watching out for the taxi. "Nixon was a big star name."

That was true enough. "Won't Barry just get a new penguin?"

She looked shocked. "You're as heartless as your old dad!"

I felt ashamed.

She went on, "Well, I don't know much about it. But I imagine it's never the same with a replacement. These puppets are unique."

I thought about Tolstoy, pushed inside my wardrobe, and I shivered. He was definitely one of a kind.

I thought about Tolstoy's damp and chilly fur.

How did he get like that overnight?

I wouldn't think about that just yet.

Mam was looking at me shrewdly over her sunglasses as she locked up the front door. "Are you keeping something to yourself, Jason?"

"No, Mam."

"Hm," she said. She looked an especially vivid green in all the deep snow. "You've been acting a bit peculiar this past day or two. . . ."

"I'VE been peculiar!" I said hotly, but we were interrupted then, by the taxi pulling up in our empty drive.

Our taxi driver never once turned to face us, but he insisted on talking to us all the way into town. From the back he looked like he could have been a werewolf. He had hair coming out of everywhere: both ears, sprouting out from under his woolly hat, up through the collar of his greasy white shirt.

His endless commentary came out in this growling, snarling voice as he put his foot down on the pedal and steered with his two meaty, hairy hands.

"The Ritzy Hotel, eh?" he said. "I wouldn't go there today. It might be the best hotel in town, but I wouldn't stay there now. Oh, no. You couldn't pay me to stay there. Haven't you seen the news this morning? I heard it on the radio, about an hour since. Imagine something like this happening in our little town! It should be a day of national mourning, that's what I think. I bet that hotel's cursed now. That's the kind of thing that can blight and curse a place forever. Why, I bet the Ritzy Hotel will be haunted now.

"That's what it's like when there's been a violent murder. Oh, I've seen this kind of thing before, and when it's a nasty case like this one, their spirits will never be at peace. Oh, I wouldn't stay at the Ritzy for any price. Oh, no. I'd not sleep where I was going to be haunted. How come you two want to go there? Haven't you heard the news?"

"Yes," said Mam, tight-lipped. "Yes, we've heard the news."

"And it hasn't put you off?" said the taxi driver. "It doesn't put you off to know that one of the country's top entertainers was brutally murdered there last night?"

"Actually," said Mam, keeping her voice very steady, "he was a relative of ours."

"Oh," said the taxi driver. He fell quiet for a bit, concentrating on his driving in the banked-up snow. Maybe he was keeping quiet out of respect. Or maybe he was imagining staying in a hotel of the plushest, uttermost luxury . . . sleeping uneasily in rooms haunted by tortured penguin souls.

"I want to know who would ever do such a thing," sighed Lisa Turmoil in the hotel lounge.

We were sitting on yellow sofas, dodging the pressmen and police in the main foyer. Out there, members of Barry's staff and representatives of his TV company were giving an official statement about the life and untimely death of Nixon the penguin. Flash bulbs were going off and there was an excited hubbub of voices.

Lisa the hairstylist looked frightened and pale. She had come straight to us and led us here, where we sat drinking coffee out of deep cups, all being shocked together.

"I mean," she said, lighting up a shaky cigarette, "I was never a big fan, or even that fond of the flipping thing, but he didn't deserve anything like this. . . ."

Mam took a cigarette off her, casually observing the details of Lisa's outfit that morning. For someone so upset, Lisa was looking pretty good, I thought. I couldn't stop staring at her.

"Where's Barry now?" Mam gently asked.

"He couldn't face the press," Lisa told her. "How could he? He's with the doctor still. There's a whole army of counselors been in with him. He and that penguin hadn't been separated in fifteen years. . . ."

"Nixon was his favorite, wasn't he?" Mam said.

Lisa nodded. "None of his other puppets came anywhere near. He has loads of others, but Nixon was his first and true love. Oh, who could do such a thing?"

She looked at us both with wet, glittering eyes. Suddenly I knew what she was thinking. Dad. She thought Dad had managed to get out in the middle of the night and come here and do this evil deed.

But that was ridiculous.

In the mirror-lined lift going to the top floor and Barry's suite, Mam seized my arm.

"Why did we let him out of his straitjacket?" she moaned. "We should have left it on him last night."

"Mam!" I gasped. "You can't think . . ."

"What else can I think? You heard him going on. You saw how he feels about puppets. And about Barry. And with the way he is now . . ."

"No, Mam," I said. "Surely not."

Lisa Turmoil was looking at us both narrowly. "If you two know anything, you'd better tell me."

I stared back fiercely. "We *don't* know anything."

Barry's suite of rooms was the most opulent and sumptuous place I had ever been. Everything was decorated in gold and maroon and it all seemed muffled and cushioned from the harshness of life outside.

We were shown into a sitting room, where Barry was

waiting, and he wasn't taking any notice of his surroundings at all. He was slumped in a velvet high-backed chair and holding one bare hand in front of his face. He was staring at his clenched fist intently, as if willing it to talk to him.

Mam went straight to him. "Oh, Barry, what a terrible thing to happen . . ."

He looked at us with pink, savage eyes. "He's gone," he said hoarsely.

"I know," said Mam.

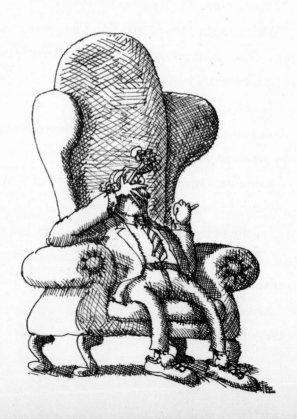

"I don't know what I'm going to do without him." He looked at his empty hand.

"But you've got lots of other friends," Mam said. "Other puppets, haven't you? Your show has to go on, Barry, for your sake. For Nixon's sake . . ."

"Don't say his name to me," Barry whimpered. "I can't bear it."

Mam nodded. "Your fans depend on you going on. . . ."

Barry wouldn't listen. "Where is he?"

"Who?"

"Dad. Didn't you bring him?"

Mam looked shifty. "He's still not well. I don't think he's ready for something like this. We left him resting at home."

Barry's face winched up in a mixture of fury and grief. "Yeah . . . we all have to make sure the old man is all right, don't we? We all have to look after the old man. Well, do you want to know what I think? I think this is all down to him."

"No, Barry!" cried Mam.

"I do! I don't know how he did it, but that nasty old sod crept in here last night and . . . and . . ."

Barry broke down in sobs.

I was staring open-mouthed.

Mam went to him and patted his tousled curly hair. "Barry, dear, you can't think that of your poor old dad. He might have his funny little ways and they might have caused a bit of bother recently . . . but he'd never do anything evil like this. Ever. You know that . . ."

Barry was crying too noisily to listen.

Mam looked at me and I could see that she was having her doubts.

Eleven

Barry wanted to have the funeral as quickly, and with as little fuss, as possible. Before Christmas, which was only a week away. He wanted his poor, murdered penguin laid to rest before their annual Christmas spectacular aired on Boxing Day. They had recorded it together in Lapland last July, and though the papers said the show would be the ratings winner of the season, Barry had decided he wouldn't watch it. It would be far too painful.

We were invited to the funeral, which was to be held on the grounds of Barry's mansion, just north of London. It would be a big trip for us, going all the way down there, but Mam didn't see how we could avoid paying our final respects to Nixon.

"Barry's house is supposed to be fantastic," Mam told me. "Real palatial splendor. Like a house that someone who won the lottery would buy."

"Bought by the wages of sin!" cried my dad from the settee. "Ill-gotten gains!"

Mam hushed him. Dad was all wrapped up in his now quite stained straitjacket. Mam fed him meals like he was a

baby. Raw carrots and broccoli florets, bananas ready-peeled. Nothing he could use to do any damage to himself, or anyone else. Nothing hot and nothing pointy.

They hadn't been able to pin anything on Dad, but the papers and TV news still mentioned his name darkly when they discussed the mysterious death of Nixon the penguin. It became well known all over the country that week that my dad was crazy. Mam thought it was best if we kept him wrapped up in his straitjacket even after the policeman had questioned him and the psychologists had probed him. All the official people had shaken their heads in puzzlement and now they left us alone.

They knew he hated puppets—and Nixon in particular—

but there wasn't a single shred of evidence against him. Whoever the penguin slayer had been, there weren't any clues left in Barry's hotel suite. It had been a very neat operation. Bits of stuffing from poor Nixon's insides had been found scattered on the carpet, and they had been examined in the most high-tech pathology labs by the most renowned experts. But nothing positive came back. It was all still a mystery.

Now the penguin's plush mortal remains were to be buried in a small private ceremony. The black-edged invitation card had arrived with our post that morning.

"But can we take Dad?" Mam hissed at me, as we ate our own raw dinner. "Would people think that was in bad taste, with him being a suspect and all?"

I shrugged. How should I know how things like that worked?

Mam was fretting, staring at Dad as he crunched his crudités, staring back at us. "I bet there'll be loads of celebrities in attendance," she mused.

Lisa Turmoil had also sent us a card that morning. It was a Christmas card showing (rather tastelessly, Mam said) a whole lot of penguins tobogganing down a hill. I thought it was nice of her to think of us, now that Barry's crew had decamped back to London and our documentary was on hold.

"Barry wants revenge," Lisa had written. "He'll stop at nothing till he knows who's to blame."

She also told us that our documentary would continue. The company wasn't about to abandon it. Anything about puppets was a sure-fire TV ratings winner. The public's interest had been at fever pitch since the death of Nixon.

"What a sick world we live in," Mam sighed. She had a notepad out, making a list of outfits she'd need to pack for the trip to Barry's. She was very organized.

"What do you think she means, about Barry wanting revenge?" I asked.

"Oh," she said. "He's just riding on a tide of public feeling."

She pushed the evening paper across the dinner table at me.

"Media whores!" barked Dad, spitting out bits of cauliflower. "Some people would do anything for publicity!"

I looked at the front-page headline:

PUPPET STARS FEAR FOR THEIR TINY LIVES!

Up and down the country tonight, puppets of all persuasions are living in awful fear of a serial killer with a crazed vendetta against them and their kind. "Nixon was just the first," said the gorgeous blonde agent to a number of top stars. "Everyone's expecting further killings at any time. This death was not just some random event. A real shockwave has rocketed through the puppet world."

"Several of our most famous performers," an insider last night claimed, "have seriously considered leaving the country since the wicked slaying of everyone's favorite penguin." "But it's the pantomime season," Wilberforce the famously saucy poodle told our reporter. "And we can't just leave on a whim, even for our own safety. We have to work, don't we? Even puppets have to eat . . ."

There was a photo of Wilberforce looking very downcast in his dark glasses, with his pompoms seeming a bit flat. He was in the arms of his buxom and underdressed mistress, Cherie. Underneath the photo it said: "Panicked but resolute . . . the poodle sticks it out."

Mam had made her mind up.

We were going and we were taking Dad. We'd face it out.

We had nothing to be ashamed of. We'd take the train down south that very night.

"Puppets come from hell!" Dad cried on the stairway. "The devil himself sends them to plague us!"

"Yes, dear," Mam said tiredly as she led him off to pack their cases.

I'd been sent to pack my stuff too.

Mam had really changed during this whole extraordinary run of events. She'd stopped being so nervous and jumpy. I sat on my bed and thought about it, with my suitcase open beside me. It was as if she'd been given a whole new lease on life.

It was the attention that had done it, I decided. Dad had locked her up in our house for years. All this recent business—however rotten and awful—had brought Mam into contact with the wider world. We were entering this world of infamy and celebrity and my Mam had discovered an appetite for it.

I'd watched her when Barry's TV crew had been filming. She'd positively blossomed.

"I'm not so sure that's a good thing," said a scratchy, sepulchral voice from the corner of my room.

I sighed. "Don't you?" I asked aloud. "No one's asking you."

The voice laughed. A nasty laugh. I could really have done without his input just now.

"Your mam's getting addicted," Tolstoy said, "to all the

attention and all the notoriety. That always happens. Your dad was just the same, the silly old goat. Your brother, Barry, too."

"Shut up," I said.

"And you want the same thing," the voice went on. "You want to be on the telly and in the papers and everything, the same as the rest of them. And you'll exploit the likes of me to get there . . . pretending we're just puppets . . . Pretending that you're the talented one!"

"I don't want to be famous!" I burst out. "I don't want to be a TV puppeteer! I don't!" I jumped up from my bed and hurried over to the wardrobe, where he was hiding under a heap of my dirty clothes. "I don't know what I want to be! I'm only thirteen!"

But Tolstoy just laughed at me.

I fished him out of hiding and gave the wretched, dirty, nasty-mouthed bat a sound shaking.

"I'm your destiny, Jason Lurcher! Hahahahahahahahaha-hahaha!"

I was sick of hearing that by now. I should never have let him out of the attic.

"But you had no choice!" he said, reading my mind. "I called and you came. Just as it was meant to be."

Tolstoy kept talking to me. It had been happening ever

since I'd liberated him from his trunk and brought him down to my room. He only talked when we were alone. I hadn't told anyone about it. I didn't dare.

"I hope you're going to pack me, along with all your things," he said suddenly. His voice had changed. Less aggressive and mocking. He sounded almost worried that I would leave him alone, while we caught the train.

"Why should I take you?" I said. "You just say horrible things all the time."

"But, Jason," said the bat, "you *have* to take me! You and me . . . we're bonded now, just like your father and I used to be. You couldn't leave me behind if you tried. . . ."

"Just you watch me," I said, pulling open a drawer and sorting through odd socks.

"But I want to pay my respects to Nixon!" he cried.

"You never knew him," I said. "He was after your time."

I looked and Tolstoy's eyes were burning with impotent rage. "I know all of the puppets!" he ranted. "And I'm as upset about the loss of Nixon as anyone!"

"Oh, yeah?"

"Yes!" Tolstoy really did sound upset. "Look," he said. "Hurt one puppet and you hurt all of us. It's our code. I have to go to the funeral. All of the most famous puppets in the country will be there at Barry's mansion. All my peers, all my old friends, all my enemies and rivals. I can't not be there, can I? You have to take me! I *have* to be there!"

I picked him up and his shiny, almost threadbare wings flapped despondently. I actually started feeling sorry for him.

"I suppose it must have been awful for you, being stuck up in the attic for twenty years," I said.

His voice was shaky when he replied. "You can't even imagine what it was like. The loneliness. The quiet. All that darkness."

"Bats like the darkness," I pointed out.

"Ha," he said. "Not bats who have known the full, neon-lit glare of celebrity. *They* don't like the darkness. The obscurity. The neglect. No, they don't like it at all." He wiped his moist snout with a wing and struggled to control his emotions.

"Well," I said, "I hadn't really thought about it like that. About what it's been like for you."

"It's been frigging awful," he said.

I smoothed down his ears and then I looked at my half-packed case.

We were getting the train in less than an hour. Mam would be calling for me soon. The taxi would be coming for us. I had to hurry up. I smoothed his rumpled, extra-long ears once more.

"Okay," I said at last.

"Okay?" said Tolstoy hopefully.

"I'll take you," I told him. "We'll go together."

He grinned and showed a whole plethora of sharp and rancid teeth. "We're a team!" he rasped, as I cleared a space in my suitcase for him. "We're going to be a real team together, Jason Lurcher!"

Twelve

We had to put an anorak on over Dad's straitjacket so no one would know he was bound up. It was Mam's idea. She didn't want to be seen on the train journey with him in "that thing." She kept calling the straitjacket "that thing," and it had become a real part of our lives. It was what kept Dad out of trouble. The sleeves of the old anorak hung down emptily while we were standing on the platform. Dad looked like he'd lost both arms in an awful accident.

We tried to keep a bit inconspicuous, standing with all our bags (Mam had brought loads of outfits). The platform was packed with people traveling home for the Christmas holidays. The station billowed with steam and the mingled smells of coffee and oil, and there was all this excitable chatter. Dad was miraculously silent, glaring about with interest.

Mam had phoned on

ahead to tell Barry when we would be arriving. In the depths of his mourning, she said, he had sounded pleased that we were coming to the do. He was having some of his guest rooms prepared ready for us.

"See?" Mam smiled at me. "Family is family, after all. Maybe something good will come out of this whole sorry business after all." She was in a polka-dotted dress and coat, with another of her big hats.

I was keeping quieter than usual, acutely aware of the suitcase at my feet. Mam had offered to sort out my luggage for me, but I'd refused to let her.

"I can pack my own stuff," I'd complained.

"Who's getting to be a big boy?" She'd laughed.

God knows what she would have said if she'd opened up my case and found the bat crushed up inside, among all my tangled clothes.

The train whooshed and snorted as it pulled up. It was chock-a-block with passengers. Mam got me to take one of Dad's sleeves to help guide him into our carriage. We both knew he hated trains even more than he hated buses. Even at his best he wasn't very good on public transport, given that he hated the public so much. But, like Mam said, we just had to grit our teeth and hope for the best.

We struggled down the gangway of the smoking carriage, looking for seats together. Mam was smoking again, taking advantage of Dad's taking leave of his senses. At last we were seated at a table that was strewn with empty cups and crisp packets and the pages of tabloid papers. We settled just as the train went shunting out of our dark, misty town. Mam lit up her first ciggie.

I'd hardly ever been out of our town in all my life. This was the first time I'd really thought about that. One way or another, the world was starting to open up for me.

Soon the train was rattling through a flat, bleak country-side. The low fields were pale with snow.

As I turned my thoughts to the trip ahead and our even-tual destination, I realized that the best thing about it would be seeing Lisa the hairstylist again. I'd missed being around her, just these past few days. What was that about?

The world had *definitely* opened up for me—and changed. When I thought back to being in the house, just me, Mam and Dad, that seemed like a different life. Some-body else's life all together.

Dad drowsed off to sleep. His great bald head sank down and soon he was muttering unconsciously, and Mam and I exchanged relieved glances. If he was asleep he couldn't cause any kind of fracas in transit.

Mam was reading her way through a heap of glossy celebrity magazines she had bought at the railway station stall. She peered critically at snaps of famous faces and their outfits at various events and outings. She read out lurid accounts of the murder of Nixon the penguin, all of which were pretty inaccurate really.

Mam wasn't usually allowed to read mags like these, just as Dad used to ration our TV viewing. But with him mostly incapacitated, Mam had embraced the real world outside, where everything was gossip, glamour and glitz.

"They're talking in here," she said, holding up this week's *HIYA* magazine, "about who's expected to go to Nixon's funeral." She frowned. "It doesn't mention us. . . ."

Suddenly Dad was awake again. It was like watching a monster come up from the bottom of the ocean. He was staring, wide-eyed, into the sleek blackness of the train windows.

"They're out there!" he wailed in a hollow, reedy voice. "Can't you see them? They're following us."

Mam looked alarmed. "Jason! Shut him up. People are looking."

"Dad . . ." I started patting his armless sleeve to no avail.

"Look out there!" he shouted, into my face. "Can't you

see them? Keeping pace with us? Flying along with the train like evil spirits . . . chasing us . . . wherever we go . . ."

"Who, Dad? What are you talking about?"

Dad was clearly in some distress. People across the gangway and in the seats behind us were taking note of his behavior and were listening in. Mam looked mortified at the way Dad was carrying on.

"Tell him to stop making a show of us," she said.

"They're out there!" Dad started to bellow, thrashing about in his seat. "Oh, why can't anyone else see them? Them, with their furry little bodies! And their beady, dead glass eyes! And their whiskers and floppy ears! Can't any of you see? Are all of you blind? They're following us wherever we go!"

There was some laughter now. Nervous giggles from the other passengers in the fuggy, fumy smoking carriage.

"Puppets! Puppets! Evil marionettes and glove puppets!" Dad howled, trying feebly to free his bound arms. "They'll murder us all! They won't rest till we're all of us dead!"

The ticket collector had appeared at our table. She didn't look at all pleased with the commotion Dad was creating.

"He's a little worked up," Mam said, cringing under her wide-brimmed hat.

"You fools," Dad said, still staring at the black windows, into the empty fields.

The inspector was checking our tickets.

Then Dad passed out in his seat.

"Well, that's something," Mam said, turning her page. "He can't embarrass us any more."

As the ticket collector waddled away satisfied, I was starting to think that my mam had turned a bit heartless of late.

When we got to King's Cross the press were waiting for us.

"Well!" cried Mam, all breathless, as the train pulled up under the high, soot-blackened arches and she shoved her head out of the window to survey the crowd. "That's more like it."

"How are we going to get Dad through that lot?" I asked her, but she didn't reply.

There seemed to be dozens of them, all lined up on the frosty platform, armed to the teeth with notepads, Dictaphones, cameras, and those microphones that look like small hairy dogs stuck on the end of spears.

Dad was awake again and he looked worse than ever. *"Radio Times!"* he chanted bleakly. *"Radio Times! Radio Times!"*

For a second, Mam's face creased in concern. "He thinks he's famous again. He thinks his glory days have come back . . ."

As we prepared to brave the press, I was left to organize all of our luggage. A small, husky voice came into my head as I bent to pick up my own case. Of course I knew who it was.

"But his glory days have indeed come again," laughed Tolstoy, hidden away in all my things. "The good old days are back for all of us now. Just you wait and see."

I tried to block him out of my thoughts.

Mam led the way onto the platform. With remarkable presence of mind, she was clearing a gap for us to walk through by swinging her bulkiest case through the air and grinning madly. "No comment! No comment!" she cried. "The Lurcher family has no comment to make whatsoever!"

The journalists around us muttered and flashed their cameras and called out questions. We ignored all of them. I was carrying bags and coaxing along my lost and bewildered dad.

"Mrs. Lurcher, are you taking your husband to the funeral?"

"Mrs. Lurcher, is your husband still the prime suspect for the murder of Nixon the penguin?"

"How does it feel to be married to a maniac?"

"Has he always been bonkers, Mrs. Lurcher?"

"Has Barry forgiven his father?"

"Will your youngest son, Julian, follow in his father's footsteps?"

"Where's Tolstoy, Mrs. Lurcher? Where's Tolstoy now?"

This last, shouted question surprised us all.

"Has Tolstoy been invited as well?"

We never saw which journalist was asking this. We just pressed on ahead, out of King's Cross. Mam kept saying, "No comment! No comment!" and looking every inch the star.

Outside, in the busy main street, where the snow was falling thick and fast, there was a big car waiting for us. Luxurious, immaculate—a cream limousine, with the back door held open, ready for us to duck safely inside.

And, holding the door, grinning in welcome, was Lisa Turmoil.

She hugged us all, even Dad—who was shocked—and then she bundled us efficiently into the car.

I sat on the backseat next to her. I was holding my breath, and still feeling the pressure of that hug as we drove away through the streets.

Thirteen

Everything we had heard about Barry's fabulous mansion was true.

It had ninety-nine rooms, a swimming pool on its rooftop and a great glass dome that sat right on top and protected everyone inside from the weather.

"Just think," said Mam as we stepped out of the limousine and gazed at the front of this huge edifice. "If Barry and your dad hadn't fallen out, we could have been living somewhere like this. This could be our lives as well."

Dad looked disconsolate in his layers of straitjacket and anorak. "Where are we now?"

"I wonder if Barry will want us to stay all through Christmas?" Mam said. "It must get lonely, just him living in this massive place. And what with Nixon gone . . ."

We were miles out of London. The sleek car had whizzed us back into the countryside, and the stars were diamond bright over the acres of snowy parkland Barry apparently owned. I hadn't known he was so rich. There seemed to be a lot of money in being a puppeteer.

Lisa was leading us up the pale marble steps to the tall front door.

"The other funeral guests have been arriving all day," she warned us. "It's very busy inside."

The front-door knocker was in the shape of a penguin. She rapped it smartly and we were shown into a main hall by a gloomy-looking butler.

"Good evening, Ron," Lisa said.

The butler was dressed very smartly. On one hand he was wearing a small yellow bulldog. He held it up to his ear and frowned, listening. "What's that, Jessie? Oh, you're saying that these people are Mr. Barry's family members, are you? Well,

thank you for telling me, Jessie. We shall have to take very good care of them, shan't we?" Both the butler and the small bull-dog looked at us solemnly and they were both nodding.

We hurried Dad across the marble floor of the entrance hall before he could get worked up at the sight of the puppet. But he was in a trance, staring at the thirty-foot Christmas tree at the bottom of the staircase.

"Christmas!" Dad said. "It's Christmas!"

"Yes, dear," said Mam.

"But we were going to buy the boy a present. . . . What was it we were going to buy him, Eileen?"

There were other people about now, all dressed in black, carrying their suitcases up the stairs. They were treating the place just like a posh hotel. I recognized some of these famous faces. As she led us up the stairs, Lisa was greeting them by name. "Hello, Marigold. Hello, Tommy. Merry Christmas, Florence."

Mam and I held on to Dad's empty sleeves. A servant was bringing up our bags, though I'd refused to let go of my own case.

"Well, I never," said Mam. Her eyes were just about out on stalks. All she could say, as she took in the sight of all this luxury, was, "Well, I never."

"Cocktails at midnight in the drawing room," Lisa told us

as she pointed out which rooms were ours. We were up on the fourth floor. "Barry wants to greet all of his guests together."

"Cocktails," Mam cooed appreciatively. "He certainly likes to make his guests feel welcome."

Lisa smiled tightly as Mam and Dad went into their room. Then she showed me to mine, down the corridor. A pudgy-faced man with a halo of golden hair squeezed past us, smiling at Lisa. He had an ostrich puppet under his arm, carrying it like a set of bagpipes.

"Good evening, Derek. Good evening, Cassandra." Lisa nodded.

She unlocked a door and let me into a room with a vast four-poster bed and a window with a view overlooking miles of the snowy parkland.

"And how's Jason doing?"

I looked at her and went all tongue-tied. I was blushing, I just knew it.

"There'll be lots of time to catch up," she said, showing her dimples. "Though I'm going to be quite busy, doing everyone's hair ready for the service tomorrow. They all want to look their best. We're filming it for the show, and there'll be photographers from *HIYA* magazine."

I sat on the tapestried bed. "Are all the most famous puppets in the world here?" I asked. "All of them?"

Lisa was turning to go. "Yes," she said. "Every single one of them. The crème de la crème of the puppetry world. But don't worry. We'll keep a close eye on your dad. He won't be able to get up to any mischief."

In the drawing room late that evening there was a great fire crackling away. Swags of freshly picked holly and mistletoe hung from the mantelpiece. There was another fir tree, all lit up with a cross-looking fairy perched on top. On settees and sofas, banquettes and poufs sat a curious array of dressed-up guests, sipping brightly colored cocktails out of elaborate glasses. I didn't recognize everyone, but some were very familiar indeed.

For a funeral party it wasn't that somber. The guests were chatting away to one another and occasionally there would be tinkles and guffaws of laughter. There was music playing through hidden speakers. Christmas carols sung, if I wasn't mistaken, by Barry and Nixon the penguin. Sweet, sentimental songs. It seemed to be a Christmas album they had recorded together.

"This should not be a sad occasion," a high-pitched, fruity, rather refined voice was saying. "We should not cry over the penguin's demise. He would want us to be happy tonight. We are all together and it is nearly Christmastime."

It was a sea horse with a French accent. She was sitting in a bucket of water by the fire, beside her mistress, who was a large-boned lady in a lilac woolen suit.

"Now, Josephine," said the big lady, "we still have to be respectful and not have *too* good a time. We shouldn't have too many cocktails, should we?" The woman had three empty glasses on the coffee table beside her. She looked a bit flushed in the heat of the fire.

The bejeweled sea horse fluttered her huge eyelashes and whinnied softly.

"I do not believe in moping about. I do not think Nixon believed in it either." She flapped green-and-blue flippers gently and said, "I knew him better than most, of course. I used to know him back in the old days before any of us were famous. When we were all just starting out . . ."

"Oh, yes," said the large lady with the rosy complexion, beginning her next foaming cocktail. "That you did, Josephine, dear."

They were interrupted by a tatty-looking monkey sitting on the knee of a young man on the sofa opposite. "Didn't you and the penguin once have a thing going, Josephine?" the monkey asked rudely, rolling his eyes suggestively.

The sea horse whinnied and tossed her snout in hauteur. "I am sure I would tell you nothing about it, even if such a thing were true. A common little monkey like you."

"Common!" shouted the monkey. "Me? Common!"

"Yes, you!" Josephine jeered. "Next to me, everyone is common. I am high-born. I am descended from French aristocracy. What are you? Just some horrid little primate."

"You're a big fake," snarled the monkey. "I knew you when you were nothing."

"Pish!" said Josephine.

As the two puppets argued, tossing insults at each other across the room, their puppeteers were quiet, smiling benignly at each other and sipping their poisonous-looking drinks.

"Oh dear," sighed Lisa Turmoil, as she led Mam and me to an empty chaise longue. "Puppets! What are they like? They'll argue about anything, won't they?"

A waiter appeared with a silver tray, offering us drinks. "Well," said Mam, "I'm really glad Frank went straight off to sleep upstairs. I don't know what he'd do in a room full of puppets like this. . . . Maybe we were silly to bring him . . ."

"Barry insisted his dad be here," Lisa told her.

Mam sampled her purple drink and looked around apprehensively.

The whole drawing room was packed with puppets and their masters and mistresses. It was bewildering, trying to make out who was real and who was full of stuffing with someone's hand up them. Real or not, the puppets were the noisiest, most talkative people in that place. Cats and snakes, tapir and frogs, yeti and bears and elephants. Every kind of puppet I'd ever seen. Someone had even brought along representatives from *Galactic Patrol*, who were marionettes on strings wearing space uniforms. They walked around jerkily and didn't look at all realistic. I'd always hated that show they were on. They were so arrogant. They didn't even try to hide the strings that operated them.

Lisa nodded to the big clock on the mantelpiece.

"It's almost time," she observed.

"Time?" Mam asked.

The clock started bonging out for midnight.

"Time," said Lisa.

All the puppets looked at the golden-faced clock and a respectful silence suddenly fell upon the festive room.

"Hey, welcome, everybody," Barry said as he walked in. He looked careworn but cheerful, given the circumstances. What was more, he was wearing a Santa Claus outfit. "I'm very glad to see you all gathered here, paying your final respects to the greatest puppet of them all." He took a glass from the waiter's tray. There was a rustling and a whispering around the room as the various guests reacted to his calling the penguin the greatest.

"I'd like to propose a toast to the memory of Nixon," announced Barry, holding up his glass.

"To Nixon!" everyone joined in, tossing back their drinks. I had some kind of awful fruit juice.

In all the commotion of the toasts, I heard a little voice going through my head.

"Pah! The greatest! What a load of shite! That penguin was rubbish, everyone knows that. Look at them all, Jason. What a bunch of frigging hypocrites. None of them could stand that git when he was alive. They only spoke to him because he was the most famous, the most successful . . ."

"Shut up, Tolstoy," I said through gritted teeth as Barry came over to greet me and Mam. "Don't talk to me. . . ."

"They're all going to pay!" Tolstoy was crowing from somewhere deep in my luggage. His voice was echoing in my skull, blotting out everything else.

"All of these minging bastards are going to pay!"

Fourteen

I was used to that cold, bare room at the top of our house. I was used to that narrow bed I'd had since I was a little kid. When it was time to go to sleep that night, it took me a little while to get used to this grand four-poster bed and all the luxury. I wasn't a bit tired. I opened the thick curtains and looked out at the moonlight over acres of snow; the silvered surface of the frozen lake; the hulking mass of trees that bordered Barry's private kingdom.

I unpacked and felt very shabby in the old pajamas I'd brought from home. They had holes and frayed patches

where they'd been washed too many times. Without even thinking, I set Tolstoy on the bedside table. He was slumped there by the softly glowing lamp, looking distinctly annoyed.

"What's the matter with you?" I asked, buttoning my pajama top.

Tolstoy grunted. "Did you have a nice party without me downstairs?" he rasped. "You and Barry and all those losers. All those useless bloody puppets."

"It was hardly a party, Tolstoy. We're here for a funeral." Though, when I thought about it, all the guests down there had been treating it just like a great big party, with free drinks and everything.

"Ha," he said bitterly. "I know that lot. Any excuse to get pissed. Was that bitch of a sea horse there?"

"Josephine?"

"That's the one. Stuck-up cow."

"She's very posh," I said.

"Is she hell."

I turned back the tapestried duvet and climbed into the bed. It was like something royalty would have.

"Are you still thinking about that Lisa Turmoil?" Tolstoy asked suddenly.

"What?" I stared at him.

"I know the way you look at her. And I can read all your thoughts. I'm a part of you now, Jason, and I know all your dirty little thoughts."

"I don't have dirty thoughts," I said, and I knew I was going red again.

"Pah!" snapped Tolstoy. "You get hot and bothered every time you clap eyes on that tarted-up hairdresser."

"No, I don't." I couldn't believe I was having this conversation with a moth-eaten bit of old rag. "Don't be so rude."

"I don't blame you for fancying her," Tolstoy went on. "She's a decent bit of skirt. Big bazoombas too."

"Tolstoy!" But I was laughing by now.

"And I reckon she's got a soft spot for you, Jason."

"You do?"

"Yeah. I reckon if you were a bit older you'd be in with a chance there."

I sank down into my pillows. "I'm only thirteen. She's twenty-something, isn't she? She probably thinks I'm a daft little kid."

"I bet she doesn't," he said. "You've got a great future ahead of you, Jason Lurcher. You're going to be a great puppeteer. The greatest ever."

I was drifting off to sleep then in all the soft pillows, with Tolstoy's voice rumbling in my head.

"But I don't want to be a puppeteer," I heard myself saying.

In my dreams that night I was walking around all the rooms of Barry's mansion. I knew the place like the back of my hand.

I was wearing Tolstoy on my hand. Something I'd never done in real life. He was all animated, flexing his wings, looking about, his small feral eyes eagerly taking in the details of Barry's opulent pad. Room after room after room, with everyone asleep: every room decorated in the highest style.

Everything ready for Christmas.

And I was thinking . . . If I became a puppeteer, all this could be mine. I could be as rich as Barry. Tolstoy on the end of my arm felt as natural to me as breathing. This ragged old bat was just an extension of me, as obvious as my other hand. Or any other part of me; of this awkward, gangly wayward body. Mam always said I was growing up and strange things happen to you when you turn into a teenager and sometimes it's like your body is out of control and it isn't even yours anymore. Hormones and that, I think she meant. But I thought that was just girls. Well, now I had my own version of hormones (whatever THEY'RE meant to be) and he was a ratty old bat with satin wings and a nasty tongue.

And he was a part of me, it seemed. We were bound together now. And I don't call that a natural part of growing up.

But that's how it was. Tolstoy and me were sleepwalking together on the night before the funeral. And that felt as natural and real as anything else.

Fifteen

Barry's servants had made meticulous arrangements and had worked hard to ensure that Nixon's funeral went swimmingly. When the motley assembly of guests were led out of the mansion at nine the next morning and into the fog that draped the parkland, we saw that everything had been well thought out.

They had cut a rectangular hole in the ice of the great silver lake. The idea was that we'd all stand on the bank among the bulrushes, Barry would say a few words and then Ron the butler and a few others would slide the small penguin-sized coffin across the ice and into the freezing lake.

"I think that's a lovely gesture," Mam said, when she heard. "Sending him back to a place like where he came from."

Dad sighed at this. "He didn't come from anywhere like that, Eileen. He was . . . he wasn't a real penguin. He was a . . . a . . . puppet."

Mam looked at him narrowly. "I hope you're not going to start up any of your funny business, Frank."

He glowered at her. "How can I? I won't be able to see anything, will I?"

Dad was going to wear a blindfold throughout the

whole service. This had been Mam's idea. She thought, if he couldn't see any of the puppet guests, he wouldn't go doolally. I was amazed that he was submitting to such treatment, but he let her put the black eye-mask on him without a whimper of protest. He was still in his straitjacket too. We were fairly confident he'd be okay as we led him down the main staircase to where the solemn guests were gathering.

"This way," said Mam. "Maybe they won't realize who he is." She seemed perturbed. "I don't think your dad is that popular in the puppet world."

I felt a twinge of annoyance then. Dad should be popular, I thought. He'd done an awful lot to popularize puppets, back in his heyday. And it was true that Barry owed his colossal fortune to Dad. Dad had taught him all he knew, after all.

Down in the main hall, where we stood nervously, with Dad all bound and blindfolded, we were back among the anonymous guests and their rather less anonymous parrots, dogs, ostriches and sea horses. Even the usually chirpy and argumentative glove puppets were subdued—one of their number had been taken. They might not have all been best mates with Nixon, but he was part of their extended family.

Mam whispered to me, "It *is* all a bit daft, when you think about it."

"How?"

"All these grown men and women, pretending like their puppets are real . . . it's a bit pathetic really."

"Shush!" I gasped. "Mam! They ARE real!"

Mam frowned at me, then smiled and patted my head. "Oh, bless your heart. I forget sometimes. How you're still just a little kid."

I was furious with her. I felt the kind of boiling rage building up inside of me that Dad must feel. But I managed to keep it down.

What was the matter with me? Just a week or so ago I'd have agreed with her. They were just puppets. Just bits of cloth, filled with stuffing and sewn up. Now it was like I was being as big a weirdo as this lot, or as Dad, or Barry. I shook my head, trying to get rid of all my confused thoughts. I'd slept very deeply in that big soft bed and that had put me out of sorts as well.

Barry appeared in his black suit and we were all told to march outside, through the tall, glossy doors. Mam took both my hand and Dad's flapping sleeve. She had really gone to town on her mourning outfit. She was in a hat with a black lace mantilla hanging down as a veil. Her coat was trimmed with black feathers, as a gesture to Nixon the penguin.

"Oooh, that's lovely," said the big lady who worked with Josephine the aristocratic sea horse. She had sidled up to us and was examining Mam's costume avidly. "How lucky you are to fit inside a little number like that. I used to be able to, years ago. Not now. I'm Marjorie Staynes, by the way. And this is Josephine." She was lugging the sea horse along in her bucket of water, struggling a bit as we walked outside, down the marble steps, onto the frosty gravel.

The sea horse looked at us, fluttered her eyelashes and nodded graciously. Marjorie might have been a fat gobby old woman, I thought, but she was a marvelous puppeteer. She had both hands on the bucket and you couldn't see how she was operating Josephine at all. Suddenly I was alert to technical details like that.

"I like your outfit too," Mam said charitably, looking Marjorie up and down.

"Oh," flustered the old woman, "I look like a bag of rags next to you."

All the guests were hanging about waiting now as the servants emerged from another door, hoisting a small coffin between them. Barry was calling out instructions and most of our party had fallen into a respectful hush.

Except Dad. Even blindfolded he had recognized who

Mam was talking to. In too loud a voice he went, "Is that that blowsy old bag Marjorie Staynes?"

Mam hushed him.

Marjorie was staring at my dad, agog. "Frank? Frank Lurcher? They've let you come?"

"Of course they have!" he bellowed.

Other guests were looking now, and muttering. "So," Dad boomed, "you're still trotting out your rubbishy old act, are you?"

"Yes," said Marjorie primly. "Me and Josephine. We're still together."

"Oh, that old thing," Dad said. "Tolstoy used to hate her."

Marjorie chuckled. "It's nice to see you, Frank. And it's good to know that age hasn't mellowed you."

"Humpf."

"And I knew what they were saying about you was all lies. I knew you wouldn't really hurt a puppet."

"Humpf," he said again.

Josephine the sea horse perked up. "I think he is still a nasty old man."

"Hush now, Josephine dear," said Marjorie. "We oldies have to stick together."

Suddenly Barry was stomping over through the crowd, looking very red in the face. "Could you lot have a bit more respect please?" he said fiercely. "Eileen, could you shut Dad up? He isn't fit for decent company."

"What?" cried Dad, struggling in all his wrappings. "What did he say?"

Barry was marching off again, and barking at the pall-
bearers to follow him, out across the whitened lawns, towards
the misty lake. We all had to trot after them. Barry was in
such a foul mood that the pace was a bit faster than he'd
planned. Marjorie had to jog along with Josephine's bucket,
spilling her water.

"Oh, this is very undignified," said the sea horse haugh-
tily, rolling her eyes.

"Right!" said Barry, when we were all at the water's edge.
He directed his servants to start pushing Nixon's coffin onto
the ice, which creaked ominously. The butler was doing it one-
handed because he had his bulldog puppet on the other one.

"What was that, Jessie?" he was asking it. "Mr. Barry
wants us to push the coffin towards the hole in the ice?
Towards Nixon's final resting place, eh? Well, we shall all have
to work together, shan't we? And push hard, shan't we?"

"Just do it!" Barry yelled, spoiling the somber mood
somewhat. "Jesus! You lot are all bloody mad. Can't you do
anything right?"

Everyone was looking down at their puppets in embar-
rassment.

Barry struggled to regain his composure. "Right," he said
at last. "Dearly beloved, we are gathered here today . . ."

The servants stepped out on the ice and started pushing the coffin. It slid easily across to the neat hole, where the black water was lapping invitingly.

"We are gathered . . . ," said Barry haltingly. "To say farewell to a very good friend of mine and a very good friend to all of you. Now, the law won't regard him as a real living person or creature, because the law discriminates against his kind—as you all well know. And so we are gathered here at this private ceremony to say good-bye to the very best penguin friend a man has ever known—"

At that point, a terrible, bloodcurdling cry went up.

"Nooo!"

It came from behind us. From back at the mansion.

"Nooooo!"

Someone had flung open the front doors, wailing in horror and dismay. The ghastly cries came rolling over the lawns towards us.

"Help! Help! It's happened again!"

In sheer frustration, Barry flung down the book he'd been using instead of a Bible (it was the *Nixon and His Furry Friends 1987 Christmas Annual*).

"What the hell's going on now?" he shouted.

Everyone was craning their necks and peering back at

the house in consternation. "What is it? What is it?" puppets and puppeteers were asking alike. "Who is it?"

I looked.

"It's happened again! Murder! Murder!"

It was one of the guests in a black suit, late for the funeral. It was the young man whose puppet was that tatty-looking cheeky monkey.

"Murder!" he shrieked at all of us through the wintry mist. "Toby's been killed! Oh, please help. He's dead!"

Sixteen

It was a very nasty spectacle that awaited us in the drawing room.

All of the guests pushed and swarmed eagerly back into the house, led by the young man, who was out of his mind with grief. Mam and I shambled along behind with Dad, clutching one another.

When we got inside there was an awful moan of horror from all the puppets and puppeteers.

"Look what they've done to him!" brayed the distraught young man. He was pointing savagely at the top of the Christmas tree.

The cross-looking fairy had been replaced.

There was a dead-looking monkey stuck up there instead.

Someone had ripped open all of his seams, and dirty, spongy stuffing was leaking out. His ears had been snipped off, and he had only one glass eye left, hanging down his face on a single thread. He looked absolutely, undeniably dead. Barry was rigid with shock.

"I woke up and he was gone . . . ," sobbed the young man. "He's never left my side, ever . . . ever since he was first stitched together . . ."

Barry patted his shoulder staunchly. "I know what you're going through, Colin. It's like somebody's ripped out your heart, isn't it?"

Colin wailed.

"Fetch the monkey down from there," Barry told the butler brusquely. "He's spoiling the tree."

As Ron the butler did as he was bid, Barry was struck by a thought. "Then . . . the murderer is here! In our midst! A serial puppet killer!"

Gasps of terror went up in the crowd. Everyone clutched their puppets. And a space had opened up around our family party. All eyes were on the bound and blindfolded figure of my dad. The eyes were accusing, suspicious, blazing with hatred.

Dad recognized the tension in the air. His voice came out weakly. "What? What is it? Surely you can't think . . ."

Mam leaped to his defense. "Look at him! He's all tied up in a straitjacket! How could any of you think for one second he'd have been able to . . ." She gestured at the pitiful, horrible tableau before us all: the slaughtered monkey now lying beside the Christmas tree. "How could he have done this?"

But the puppeteers and the puppets had turned into a mob, murmuring their unreason. There was no talking to them.

"Take him!" Barry shouted. "Make sure he can't get away! Hold him down!"

As one, the crowd turned and pounced on my poor, bound Dad.

"Wait!" I shouted. "That monkey had more than one enemy in this room."

"What?" said the young man, Colin. "Toby didn't have any enemies at all. He was just an amiable, cheeky little monkey . . ."

I swung round and pointed my finger straight at the snout of the startled sea horse, Josephine. "She was arguing with him last night. In this very room. He was accusing her of being just as common as he was, and she didn't like it much. . . ."

Josephine bristled at me. All the spines stood out on her back as she rose up in indignation. "A murderess? I?"

Everyone was looking at

her strangely and Marjorie had a very funny expression on her face.

"Jason," Mam said, looking appalled.

I didn't know what had come over me. Everyone was staring. All I knew was that they had Dad wriggling and struggling in their grasp, and it wasn't fair. He couldn't have harmed Toby the monkey. He was being wrongly accused just because he was bonkers.

"Julian," Barry growled at me, "you don't know anything about it. Leave this to the grown-ups."

"I won't!" I burst out. "You just want to pin this on Dad. You planned all this, Barry. That's why you invited him to the funeral, I bet. I bet you murdered that monkey yourself, just to get my dad locked up!"

This accusation caused another flurry of excitement and another wave of angry protest from the mob.

"Oh, Jason!" Mam was shouting. "You can't . . ."

"Silence!" Barry roared. "I will not be accused of heinous crimes in my own home!"

But I wouldn't stop. "You planned all of this. You want revenge on my dad."

All eyes were on Barry. "I didn't plan this, Julian. Hey, hey." His voice softened, but I still didn't trust him an inch, even though his eyes were wet with tears. "I couldn't hurt a puppet, even an irritatingly cheeky one like that monkey. You know that. But our father is insane, Julian."

"No!" Dad shouted out, still trying to free himself of his captors. "I'm the only sane one here! You are all fools. Blind fools. You can't see what the puppets are up to? They're taking you over. They want to take over the whole, entire world!"

Barry gave a bleak laugh. "Listen to that. Now tell me he's in his right mind."

I couldn't.

Barry clicked his fingers. The drawing-room doors opened and two evil-looking men wearing white coats and rubber gloves came shuffling in.

"The law won't recognize what our father has done as a serious crime. Puppets have no legal status and they won't lock him up. So . . . I have decided to take the law into my own hands. . . ."

The two white-coated men were taking control of Dad. He was rigid with shock. "What's happening?" he asked in a high-pitched, terrified voice.

"Help!" shrieked Mam. "Who are they? What are they doing to Frank?"

"He'll be safe," said Barry commandingly. "They're taking him to a private asylum. A place not many people know about. Somewhere outside the usual system."

"What?" Mam was confused. "Frank, come back . . ."

Dad had relaxed into the care of the two sinister, efficient strangers. They were carrying him out of the room between them. "Eileen." He was moaning. "Eileen, save me. . . ."

"Where?" Mam asked, clawing at her black lace veil. "Where are they taking him?"

Barry told us and everyone in that room gasped.

"To the Light Entertainment Sanatorium," he announced. "It's an asylum for the criminally and formerly famous. He'll be very happy there. It's terribly exclusive. None of your hoi polloi. Only the most famous loonies get locked up there."

Barry looked on, nodding with approval as our dad was hauled away.

The rest of us were numb with shock.

Toby the monkey was lying forgotten at the foot of the Christmas tree.

They tried to get things to settle down after that. Nixon's funeral had been eclipsed by the horror of Toby's sudden death. The servants carried the shredded monkey away and some of the guests looked after the inconsolable Colin.

The somber, respectful quiet of the day had been ruined. Mam and I had rushed outside, just in time to see Dad being locked into the back of a big white van. The two white-coated doctors hurried round to the front and drove off quickly, before we could get anywhere near. The van had THE LIGHT ENTERTAINMENT SANATORIUM emblazoned in colorful letters on its sides. I managed to read it before they sped off, leaving burning rubber on the gravel of the drive.

"They've taken him!" Mam screeched. "Oh, Jason . . . what are we going to do without him?"

In a weird way, it was good to see that Mam was bothered about Dad.

"Good riddance," Barry said, behind us.

Mam rounded on him. "You had no right. . . ."

"I had every right!"

"You planned this. Your revenge . . ."

"My revenge," he said. "And Nixon's."

"I'll never forgive you, Barry," she said.

"I think you will, Eileen."

"Pah," she said, in a voice oddly like my dad's. Then she stalked back into Barry's mansion and up to her room.

Barry looked at me. "That should make quite a good shot."

"What?"

He nodded to the camera crew by the marble fountain. I couldn't believe it. He'd had the whole thing filmed for his lousy documentary. Dad's being taken off to the asylum and everything. He'd planned every bit of it.

"You're the evil one," I told my older brother. "You killed that monkey. It's all down to you."

He looked serious. "Honestly, Julian. I didn't. I wouldn't do something like that, no matter how much I wanted our dad locked up."

"Pah," I said. "Anyway, my name's Jason, not Julian. You can't even get that right, you fat, talentless git."

"Talentless?" he shouted. "Talentless?"

I looked him up and down. "Your lips used to move when Nixon was talking. You're a shite ventriloquist, Barry. Absolutely shite."

Barry stood there, frozen in apoplexy on the marble stair.

I stomped past him, bitterly satisfied, back into the house, where the guests were still milling and gossiping.

Lisa Turmoil stopped me at the bottom of the staircase. She looked flustered, her hair all awry. "What do you think you're doing, Jason? Accusing Barry! Causing bother!" Her face was flushed quite attractively. I tried to block that out of my thoughts.

"It's not me causing bother," I said sulkily, and walked past her. Usually I looked forward to talking to her. Now I was too cross and confused.

She caught my arm. "Jason . . . there's something going on, isn't there? Something bad."

I nodded. "Yes."

"And you know more about it than anyone, don't you?"

"No!" I shouted. "How can you chuck questions at me at a time like this? They've just dragged my dad off! They've driven him off to God knows where."

"I know," she said, biting her lip. "But if you do know anything . . . if anything was wrong . . . you'd tell me, wouldn't you?"

I looked at her. I thought: grown-ups! They're not to be trusted. They're all two-faced and bonkers in the end.

"Yeah," I said.

Lisa leaned forward and kissed me on the cheek. "Good boy," she said, and then she hurried off to find Barry.

I turned away, my face scalding red. I ran up the four flights to my room.

I stood looking out of the window for a bit at all the snow.

Then I turned and picked up Tolstoy. His lusterless eyes gazed back at me knowingly. I took a deep breath and, because I knew I had to, slid my hand up inside of him. And then he really did come to life.

Seventeen

So many people have got it coming to them. That's what Tolstoy is thinking.

I know because I can hear him thinking. His thoughts travel straight into me.

So many people have got to pay for all these years of neglect to Tolstoy. And now they're going to get their comeuppance.

The Good, the Bat, and the Ugly

Tolstoy was the greatest. The most lifelike. His eyes used to light up green. He'd flap his sheeny purple wings. He had an answer for everything and they brought him down when he was at his best. When he was at the height of his powers.

Well, now he's coming back.

Better watch out, world.

The guests at Barry's mansion were making their excuses and leaving early. Not even the lure of Barry's generous hospitality could keep them under his roof. The whole place was cursed now, as far as puppets were concerned. We were all steeped in the shadow of that dead cheeky monkey.

I could hear them on every level of the house, slamming doors and hurrying down the stairs with their bags and their puppets stashed safely away. Cars and taxis were pulling up on the drive to take the puppeteers to the railway station. The dignity and planned solemnity of the day had been forgotten, just as Nixon the penguin had been, as he sank through the chilly waters of the silver lake.

Mam came knocking at my bedroom door round about tea time. I put Tolstoy hurriedly away in my suitcase. I realized now that no one must know about his return to life. Not yet. He was my terrible secret and there was something deli-cious about that.

Mam was tear-stained and puffy-eyed. She had great black fronds of mascara running down her face. I hugged her. Sometimes she did daft things, but she was still my mam.

"They won't even tell me the address of this asylum they've sent your dad to," she moaned.

"Barry thinks he can do anything because he's got loads of money," I said.

"It's true," she sniffed.

"Do you want to go home?" I asked.

"Without your Dad?"

"We can't stay here," I said, remembering what I'd called Barry before I stomped upstairs.

Mam's eyes had gone a bit crafty. "I think I've got a plan," she said.

Uh-oh, I thought. I dreaded to think what a plan of Mam's might be like when she was in this state.

"You know Barry's still making this documentary, all about your dad's descent into puppet-related madness?"

I nodded. "He was filming Dad being taken away in the loony van."

Mam shivered. "Well, he wants to edit it and put it all

together ready for Christmas Eve. He wants to show it then—and he's got the TV networks to agree—as a special *Tribute to Nixon* show."

"That's awful," I said. Dad was going to be a laughing-stock. He'd never be let out of the asylum when everyone saw what he was like.

"We'll just have to bear it," Mam said. "But Barry also wants me and you to go on the live segment of the show, to discuss all the recent tragic events."

"Live on Christmas Eve?"

She nodded. "And if we're on live, we can say what we want, can't we? Barry can't stop us. We can say what a kind, loving father and husband Frank is, and how he isn't really the puppet killer they think he is. And then the whole country will know the truth. And then they'll just have to let him go."

I looked at her. "That's your plan, Mam?"

"What do you think?"

I thought it was rubbish. I couldn't say that, though. She'd be devastated. It was the best she could come up with under the circumstances.

"I think it's a great idea," I said, pretty flatly.

"Good," she said. "We have to plan what we'll say and

get it right and not let on to Barry or anyone. We'll have to play along with how he wants things to be."

"Okay," I said.

Then I could hear Tolstoy's voice, whispering, at the back of my head.

"This is brilliant! This is fantastic! Live TV! Live TV! Live TV here we come!"

Eighteen

One of the few guests brave or stupid enough to hang around Barry's mansion in the days after the monkey murder was Marjorie Staynes. She took up almost permanent residence in the Christmassy drawing room (the very scene of the ghastly crime) and sat knitting with spangly mohair wool. All the time she was tutting and shaking her head. She also spent a lot of time with Mam, the two of them drinking sherry on the fat sofa as the snow fell past the windows and the days inched along towards Christmas Eve.

None of us saw much of Barry. He kept whizzing out in his silver limousine, off to London to supervise the editing of the footage for the documentary. I felt sure he would make Dad look like a complete maniac. They might as well chuck away the key.

So I was left to my own devices for a while, as Mam cemented her friendship with the plump and interfering Marjorie. Josephine the sea horse sat in her bucket on the floor and chipped into their conversations occasionally, but, as usual, she liked to look as if she was aloof from most things.

I wandered through the many rooms of the mansion. When I went into some of them, they were already familiar from my dream. I kept seeing Lisa Turmoil around the place, going about her business along with Barry's other staff. She looked so cool and organized. She was the youngest of Barry's employees, but she was still older than me. At school, even girls my own age wouldn't look at me. But Lisa had. She talked to me like a grown-up and I liked that. I was used to spending my time with grown-ups and they'd always seemed like another species to me. Lisa didn't though. With her dimples and her snub nose, she seemed less strange to me than the kids at school and the adults around me.

On those days before Christmas I'd pass her in the main hallway or on the stairs and she'd be carrying her hairbrushes or hot tongs and at first she was a bit off with me, a little bit frosty. Maybe I had been a bit rude to her, after all her help and everything. But I'd been upset! My dad had been carried off.

Eventually I managed to apologize. I was about to pop in on Mam in the drawing room, when I saw Lisa coming out with her arms full of hairdressing supplies.

"Oh, hello," she said. "I've just been giving Marjorie a quick shampoo and set. We're working on hairdos for the broadcast tomorrow night."

"Marjorie's going on the telly as well?" I asked. "With us?" Lisa nodded.

"With that stupid sea horse puppet?"

Lisa said, "They were both witnesses. They were here when Toby the monkey died. They've got a story to tell and they're always very popular with the public."

I rolled my eyes. Then I changed the subject. "I want to say I'm sorry, Lisa," I said, a bit humbly. "If I snapped at you the other day . . ."

She waved a jumbo-sized can of hairspray airily. "Never mind about that." She laughed. "I can take a tantrum or two. I work with Barry, remember."

I smiled. "I don't want to spoil us being friends." I looked down.

She punched my shoulder. "No way, kiddo. We're mates, right? We were mates the first time I came round your house. That's just how it is."

My heart was pounding away. I grinned. "You see, the thing is, Lisa . . ."

"What?" She laughed. "Don't be tongue-tied, Jason. What is it?"

"I really fancy you. . . ."

She stared. Her eyes went dead wide. "You what?"

I couldn't say it again. I tried, but I couldn't.

Now she was laughing at me. "You fancy me! Is that what you said?"

I looked down. My face was burning.

Lisa punched me in the shoulder again. "Why, you mucky little devil! Hahahahahahaha! He fancies me! Hahahahahahahahahahahahahaha! What are you? Eleven? Twelve?"

"Thirteen," I mumbled.

"Thirteen!" She laughed. "Hahahahahahahaha! God, thanks a lot, Jason. Now I really feel over the hill! Hahahaha-hahahaha!"

Then she went wandering off down the corridor, still laughing her head off. "See you later," she called, without even turning round.

She'd reacted like it was all a big joke.

I stood still for a while, outside the drawing room.

Bloody hell.

I'd show them all.

* * *

In the drawing room Marjorie Staynes was still knitting away in purple glittering mohair wool. Mam was glugging back treacly sherry. Josephine the sea horse seemed to be in a huff. When I stepped into the room none of them took one bit of notice.

Marjorie was knitting a purple monkey. She'd got on so far with it you could tell what it was now. She was on with the head and the rest of it hung down, all floppily.

"Do you knit all your puppets, Marjorie?" Mam asked. Her voice was a tad slurred in the dusk of late afternoon.

"Of course," said Marjorie. "Though this one isn't for me. It's for that poor young man who's now monkeyless. I'm making him a new one."

"That's nice," said Mam.

"It probably won't be the same." Marjorie sighed. "I don't know what I'd do if I lost Josephine."

The sea horse snorted with derision.

"Did you knit Josephine?" asked Mam.

The sea horse squealed in horror.

Marjorie hushed Mam. "You'll hurt her feelings. But yes, I did. Many years ago, when my poor old fingers were much more nimble. I'd never manage all those fiddly bits these days."

The sea horse's spines were quivering.

"It's a very pretty sea horse," Mam said. "And, really, I think it's incredible, the way you can still operate her, even while you're knitting with both hands." Mam was frowning in concentration. "And the puppet's standing in a bucket over there and on the carpet."

"Shush!" said Marjorie. "I'm not operating her. She's real, of course!" The plump woman gave a nervous laugh. "Honestly, Eileen, you don't know anything about good manners around puppeteers. We never draw attention to things like that. It's very rude."

"I'm sorry . . . ," said Mam.

"You'd never think you'd been married to a great puppet master. You seem completely ignorant." Marjorie came to the end of a row and bit through a strand of wool with her false teeth.

"I am," Mam said sadly. "Frank wouldn't talk about his old life when he was with me. His old life among all the puppets."

Marjorie cast on again. "In a way, you're lucky. It's a complicated world, the world of the puppets. You're best out of it. It's worse than having kids, though I've never actually been blessed with children. Kids grow up, you see, and then they're off your hands. They're adults, out in the world."

Both women turned and looked at me a bit sadly.

"But puppets," said Marjorie, clacking her needles methodically, "well, you take up the care of a puppet and you've got them for life. They don't grow up. They don't stop needing you. You're together for the rest of your lives. . . ."

Mam pursed her lips. "Frank managed it. He put Tolstoy away. He put him in the attic and forgot all about him. And that was an end to it."

Marjorie Staynes gave a short, bleak laugh. "You really believe that, do you? That it's as easy as all that?" She shook her head and her needles clicked busily. "It's not, Eileen. It never is. That bond will stay forever. They've been connected all that time and you never knew it. And, in my humble, old woman's opinion, that's what's driven your poor Frank doolally. He's in denial. He's in denial of his long-eared bat."

Mam looked startled. "Poor Frank," she said. "He did it all for me." She looked at me. "For this one too. For Jason. He tried to leave his old life behind."

"No one can," said Marjorie sagely. "Eh, Josephine?"

"So, you are talking to me now, are you?" sniffed the sea horse. "After talking all about me behind my back and saying that I am knitted, like some kind of jumper or an old pair of socks? Well, I am not to be talked about like that. I am important! I am the most important person in this room!"

"Yes, yes, dear," said Marjorie, smiling. "Of course you are."

That night there was a terrible fracas in Marjorie's bedroom. It was on our floor of Barry's mansion, just a few doors down from my room. When the shrieks and cries broke out everyone came running.

The sea horse was lying on the deep pile of the carpet. Her bucket had spilled its water everywhere. Josephine was shaking and shivering and gibbering in fright. All of her dignity was gone. We were kneeling around her as she feebly moved her spines and her eyes rolled in their sockets.

"Josephine," said Marjorie, patting her gently. "What is it? What happened?"

"I was attacked," she whinnied. "In the dark! Out of nowhere! I was attacked in the middle of the night!"

"But I didn't see anything," said Marjorie.

"You were asleep, you stupid old woman," snarled the sea horse. "But I tell you—I was ravished. I managed to fight the creature off, though. My cries brought all of you running and my assailant fled. Luckily! Otherwise I too would be dead by now."

"But who did it?" Mam asked her. "Who did this to you?"

"I just saw a shape," said Josephine. "It was very dark. It was very confusing. But I know . . . that I saw wings . . . beating at me . . . slashing at me . . . and pointy little teeth . . ."

"Wings?" I said.

"Shiny wings . . . ," she said. "And two large . . . two large furry ears . . ."

Josephine's voice faded away and she started shaking again. She was in shock after her brush with death.

Mam and I looked up from her slowly and then we stared at each other in dread.

And I realized what it was that I was hiding behind my back.

Nineteen

We'd forgotten all about Christmas. I felt awful when I woke up the next morning because I'd not remembered to buy presents or anything. Life had kind of got in the way. Mam hadn't said a word about it either. We'd been more focused on going on Barry's live broadcast on Christmas Eve. Mam was still convinced she could slip in a good word for Dad once we got on the telly, but I wasn't so sure.

I couldn't see how it would be a very Christmassy show, with Barry going on about Nixon and all the puppet murders, but anyway. People like to watch all sorts of strange things.

For once, Barry joined us at breakfast on the morning of Christmas Eve.

This was in his dining room, which had this really long, highly polished table in it. All the breakfast things were laid out on silver platters—bacon, mushrooms, fried eggs.

Mam looked queasily at her bowl of muesli and sunflower seeds. "I don't think I can hold anything down. I'm sick with nerves."

Today Barry was Mr. Showbiz again, powering up for his show tonight. He was in a black kimono and he was being all hearty. "Worried about your TV debut, Eileen? I wouldn't be. You're a natural in front of the camera. I've seen the footage of the documentary, remember."

Mam blushed. "Am I? A natural?"

"Hey, well, yes, of course."

She beamed at him and looked a lot less sick.

"Actually," Barry went on, "I might have a little proposition for you, Eileen . . . if the show tonight goes well . . ."

"Oh, yes?"

Barry tapped his nose waggishly. "I think you might have a future in TV presenting ahead of you!"

Suddenly my mam was radiant. She positively glowed with pleasure, all the way to the roots of her hair. She took a deep breath and exploded. "Jason! Did you hear that? Did you?"

"Yes, Mam," I said, glaring at Barry.

"I'm going to be a star. Your brother, Barry, is going to make me a TV star!"

"Hey," he said, laughing, "calm down, Eileen. You can't become a star overnight, you know. But if we started you off small scale, maybe on something like . . . I dunno . . . a show where you go round people's houses and redecorate their front rooms . . . or their gardens. Or maybe something where you show them how to paint watercolor portraits of their pets . . . or give the pets makeovers . . ."

Mam clapped her hands. "That would be amazing."

"Well," said Barry, toying with his scrambled eggs and kipper. "You play your cards right on the live show tonight and we'll just see, hey?"

Mam fell on her muesli with gusto.

I narrowed my eyes at Barry. He was up to something, I knew it. I hoped he wasn't just building my mam's hopes up for nothing. I knew how much she loved the telly and dreamed of being on it.

"Oh, Barry," she said to her stepson, "that's the best Christmas present anyone could ever give me. . . ."

We drove to the television studios in Barry's limousine. The silver van was behind us, with all of Barry's personal helpers inside. Lisa Turmoil was in there, armed with her usual brushes and clippers and gallons of hairspray. I was trying to act normal with her and carry on as usual. But I couldn't help still feeling stung for the way she'd laughed at me. In her eyes I was just a daft kid. Well, we'd see about that. I decided to say nothing much to her.

As we'd climbed into the limo we'd caught a glimpse of Barry's other puppets, being loaded into their van in their protective trunks. Since the death of Nixon they had been under close guard, twenty-four hours of the day, like members of the royal family. Which is ridiculous, when you think about it, because they were just Bertie the turtle, Sandy the pig and some other thing (I could never work out what kind of animal it was meant to be). These were Barry's second favorites. They always made appearances on his shows, but they were always second to the late, lamented penguin. I was never very impressed by them.

I had my sports bag with me, and Tolstoy was pressed down inside, hidden away underneath my clothes for the live broadcast. I'd brought him, even after the row the two of us had had in the very early hours of that morning. It had been after I'd returned to my room, just after Josephine the sea horse had woken us all up.

"She said she was attacked," I told him. "By something with shiny wings, pointed teeth and two big furry ears!" I'd picked him up and was shaking him soundly.

"I wonder who that could have been," he rasped as I throttled him. He was just trying to keep his cool and sound hard.

"It was you!" I shouted. "It's all been you, Tolstoy! All of it! And Josephine managed to survive and she saw you."

"Yeah, yeah." He snickered.

I sank onto the bed in horror. "Oh, God. It all makes sense. You killed the penguin and then the monkey. And you saw to it that Dad took all the blame. You've been after revenge the whole time. Why didn't I see? I've been really stupid. . . ."

Tolstoy was gazing back at me, all innocent. His beady eyes gleamed. "But I never go anywhere without you, Jason. I can't, can I? I'm just a puppet."

"You're not just a puppet," I said.

"Oh, but I am. That's what anyone sensible would think."

I punched him in the furry stomach and, of course, he didn't feel it.

"Puppets can't do anything by themselves," he said. "That's obvious. Anywhere I've been, you've been, Jason. So if I'm guilty, then you are too."

"Me?"

"Yes, you, Jason. Do you remember running to Josephine and Marjorie's room tonight? Hm? Or do you just remem-ber standing there, all of a sudden, and then the sea horse screaming?"

"I . . . I don't know . . ."

"Memory blackouts," he said smugly. "Oh dear."

164

"Are you saying I could have murdered Nixon and Toby the monkey and then blanked it out of my mind?"

Tolstoy shrugged. "One of us is doing it, Jason. Maybe we're both as guilty as each other . . ."

I was terribly confused and overwhelmed by now. I fell back asleep and tried not to have any dreams at all. When I woke, in time for breakfast, Tolstoy was still sitting there.

"Are you still taking me to the TV studio?" he asked.

"W-what will you do if I don't?"

He smiled. "I don't think you want to find out. But I could get you into a lot of trouble, Jason."

I didn't doubt it. "I think you already have."

I started to pack my stuff.

"Look at it this way," he said. "A few more famous puppets out of the way and more job opportunities come up, don't they? The whole world is full of sickly sweet nicey-nice puppets. Your old dad was right. What a bunch of soft gits. They're not a patch on me. If we bump a few more off, then they have to let me back on the telly."

I stared at him. "My dad wouldn't want to go back on the telly with you."

"Not him." The long-eared bat shook his head. "Your dad's too old and crazy. And Barry's a shite puppeteer. I'm talking about you, Jason. I'm talking about your future career. You and me together, Jason. Broadcasting to the whole nation on Saturday nights . . ."

"My future career . . . ," I echoed.

"That's right," said Tolstoy. "I'm about to make my comeback at last. So shove me in your bag. Smuggle me onto the show."

I did as I was told.

I wasn't in my right mind.

All I know is that it seemed the right thing, what that bat was telling me to do. It seemed the only thing to do. So he was coming to the studios with us, as that stately silver limo glided through the snowy countryside on Christmas Eve.

We were headed for London and another shot at fame.

They let us in through the special entrance at the back.

It was a huge, imposing building with windows of smoky glass. Some bloke in a Nazi uniform came out of his little hut, waved at Barry and opened the gates.

"We're actually going into Transmission House," Mam cried. "I can't believe it!"

"Oh, it's not so exciting," yawned Marjorie Staynes. "You get used to it. I've been coming here for thirty years."

"And I myself am ever so blasé," said Josephine.

"Hey, don't spoil it for Eileen and the kid," Barry told

them. "Being on TV is a big new thing for these guys."

"It'll be like going to heaven," said Mam softly. "I just know it."

The limo and the silver van parked up in special places in the car park and everyone clambered out a bit stiffly after the long drive. Barry clapped me on the back and we stood looking up at the huge building where the studios lay.

"What do you think, kid? This is the place where all those great old TV shows were made. All of them, in here. All those fabulous, famous puppets first appeared here, and a lot of them are still going."

"Really?" I asked.

"Sure. The whole building is teeming with puppets. Specially tonight, on Christmas Eve. Many of them will be here for my show." It was true. On Barry's live show he always had lots of famous puppet faces in the studio audience.

A whole building full of puppets . . .

Tolstoy was whispering away in my head. I tried to block him out.

"You're not nervous about the show, are you, Julian?"

"Of course not," I lied.

"Have you ever thought about going into the family business yourself?" Barry asked me suddenly.

"Me?" I asked. "No. I don't know what I want to do with my life."

Mam butted in, her face still aglow with excitement. "His poor dad wanted to buy him his first puppet for this Christmas. That's what they were going to buy, the day that poor Frank . . . was unwell."

"His own puppet, eh?" Barry chuckled, patting me on the back again. "We'll have to see what we can do about that."

He started leading his company of helpers and guests into the entrance of Transmission House, home of the greatest puppet shows of all time. Barry acted like he owned the place.

And I was thinking . . . I've already got a puppet of my own.

I've got one already and, as yet, no one knows.

Tolstoy is mine!

Twenty

We were taken deeper and deeper into the narrow white corridors of Transmission House and it was like a labyrinth inside. You'd never be able to find your way back out unless someone helped you. While Barry went off to do technical things with his crew, Lisa Turmoil led us guests to our dressing rooms.

All the white walls of the corridors had framed photos of famous puppeteers of the past. All of them were holding up their puppets and grinning madly at the camera.

"Oh, look," Mam cried out suddenly. "Look, Jason!"

It was Dad, in a glossy color eight-by-ten. He looked much, much younger in the photo. His hair was even black and combed back with Brylcreem. He was in a purple velvet evening jacket and bow tie. The smile on his face didn't look evil or fake at all. He looked happy and hopeful, his whole future in front of him. On his arm, Tolstoy the long-eared bat was groomed and tidy. He didn't look at all scraggy and malevolent. He even seemed like the kind of puppet it was safe for kids to watch. He was smiling and spreading out his satiny wings, which were clean.

"Oh," said Mam. "Your dad's younger here than we've ever known him, Jason."

"Yeah," I said.

"That's what he looked like when I used to watch him on the telly," said Mam. "Back when I was a little girl."

I'd never thought about that. That Mam might have seen Dad on the telly when she was a kid. She noticed my odd expression.

"I used to love Tolstoy the bat," she smiled. "He was my favorite. Because he was naughty and he answered back and said everything he wasn't supposed to say. That was before it all went wrong, of course."

"Isn't it weird," Lisa asked, "to marry someone you knew from watching the telly?"

I looked at her. She was so involved in our lives now. It was making me blush, just being around her. I would have to stop that. She thought I was just a kid.

"Weird?" said Mam. "Not at all. Telly is the realest thing in the world—that's what I've always thought. It just seemed natural to me, to find and marry my favorite TV person. Anyway, it's not as if I married the puppet, is it? It's not like I married the bat."

Both women laughed then and we went into the tiny dressing room Mam and I had to share.

The two of them and Marjorie started fussing on about outfits and hairstyles and stuff, and I knew they would be at it for ages. Mam was changing all her plans for how she wanted to look on the show tonight. She wanted to make an extra special effort after what Barry had said.

"Do you really think he'll make me a star, Lisa?" she asked, as Lisa combed through her hair.

"He can be a real show-off," said Lisa. "But he's got a lot of power too. So maybe he means it."

"I hope so," Mam said, gazing at her own reflection. I just knew that she was imagining herself on the telly. She'd picked up one of Lisa's hairbrushes and was using it as a microphone.

I said, "I'm going to have a wander round and explore."

"Don't go too far, Jason!" Mam shouted. "Don't you get lost and go shaming me."

"No, Mam." I knew that she'd quite like to have a poke round Transmission House herself. It was like the place all of her dreams came from. But for now, her hairdo and nails were the most important things. I seized my opportunity and slipped out. I took my sports bag with me and nipped off down the corridor. It was a relief to be away from the hairspray smell of Lisa. I didn't want to think too much about her. I had other things I needed to concentrate on and it felt like I was in a dream.

* * *

It was a little like being in a huge hospital. There were people stalking about holding clipboards, looking very busy and pre-occupied. There were signs on all the walls, pointing the way to different reception areas, waiting rooms, dressing rooms and studios. No one took any notice of me as I wound round corner after corner, through hundreds of sets of double doors. They were all too important to notice some little kid on his own. Soon I was lost in the heart of the place, and that suited me fine.

I came to this café where there were a few fat fellas in business suits slurping at tiny cups of coffee and a woman stood behind a counter with loads of bars of chocolate laid out. It didn't look like a very clean café. I was about to move on when I saw, sitting at a grubby table by himself, the man with the pudgy face and golden hair who'd been at Nixon's funeral party. He was holding his ostrich puppet under one arm and its gangling legs were hanging down. The man was eating a cheese-and-pickle sandwich.

"Hello," he called out to me. "Aren't you Barry's little brother? Are you here for his show tonight?"

I went over. "I am," I said.

"I'm Mr. Derek," he said. "And this is Cassandra, my ostrich."

The stuffed bird lifted her beak up and glared at me balefully and then she gave a stiff little nod. "We're going to Barry's show as well," Mr. Derek said. "We're going to join him onstage at the end for the final sing-along." He scowled. "We're not very keen, to tell you the truth."

"Didn't you used to have your own show?"

Mr. Derek's face clouded. "Once upon a time we did. But then we were axed. Now it's just odd guest appearances. A bit of daytime TV. We get on talk shows sometimes. We went on the *NANCY!* show once to talk about the perils and pitfalls of showbiz."

"I bet there's a lot of perils in showbiz," I said.

"Oh, there are," said Mr. Derek. "One day they all love you. Then they're saying all the kiddies are frightened of your puppet. You're not thinking of going into the business, are you, young man?"

I shrugged. "Barry thinks I should. I've got the puppeteering gene in me."

The pudgy-faced man snorted. "Poor you." He narrowed his twinkling eyes.

"Have you got a puppet of your own?"

I was about to say no. Then a daring thought jumped into my head. "Yes," I said.

"Then you're doomed to a life of it," sighed Mr. Derek. "There's no getting away." He looked resentfully at his ostrich and the ostrich stared back. "I'm stuck with her."

Cassandra snarled at him.

I put my sports bag on the mucky café table. "He's inside here."

"Oh," said Mr. Derek.

"He's keen to go on Barry's show tonight, with me," I said. "But I'm not sure it's a good idea."

The café around us was emptying out. The suited men had left, no doubt bustling off to some meeting. Even the woman in the pinny at the counter called out to us, "Would you mind watching the till for me, loveys? I've just got to nip to the loo. I'm bursting."

We nodded at her.

Mr. Derek lowered his voice. "One day soon you'll find

that what you really want doesn't matter a jot." He nodded at my sports bag. "That creature in there will get his own way all the time, every time. Once you've got a puppet, your life isn't your own."

Then Mr. Derek was hoisting himself off his stool. "Now, if you'll excuse me, I have to go to the lavatory too. Would you mind watching my ostrich for me?"

I was being left in sole charge of the small café. My heart was thudding and I didn't know why. "Aren't you taking her with you?"

Mr. Derek looked aghast. "Take Cassandra to the gents with me? Don't be ridiculous. She'd be mortified." Then he hurried out, through the glass door.

We were left alone. Cassandra the ostrich lay slumped on the table, among the spilled sugar and slopped tea.

I unzipped my sports bag. The zip sounded strangely loud in the empty café.

I pulled Tolstoy out into the open, coffee-scented air. "Transmission House!" he cried, gnashing his tiny teeth. "I'd know it anywhere! I feel like I've come home at last!"

I stroked his matted, ruffled hair.

He snarled when he saw Cassandra the ostrich lying there. "Look at that raggy old thing. She was a useless puppet. I hated her." He flapped his wings in irritation.

"Mr. Derek's just gone to the loo," I said. "So has the waitress."

"Then we'll have to be quick," Tolstoy growled. "Won't we?"

I didn't say anything else. Between us we picked up the floppy ostrich and hurried over to the counter, where the coffee was percolating and the till lay unattended. But we weren't interested in the money. We weren't common criminals.

We opened the heavy door of the microwave oven. Usually it was used to heat up pasties and sausage rolls. Now, though, we were bundling the hairy body and ropey legs of the ostrich inside. It took some doing, but we managed to cram in all of Cassandra. I slammed the door.

"Hahahahahahahahahahaha!" went Tolstoy.

I dithered over the control buttons.

Through the door you could see the helpless bird's staring eyes.

"Thirty seconds should do it!" Tolstoy shouted.

I pressed the buttons and the lights inside the microwave came on and then Cassandra the ostrich, all bundled up, started to steam. The steam spiraled up in smoky tendrils from her lumpy body as she went on going round and round and round . . .

Twenty-one

Ping!

That's the sound a dead puppet makes. *Ping! Ping!*

The noise of a microwave switching off and the light going out.

Ping! Ping! Ping!

Of course, we barely heard it. We were running away, out of the staff canteen, before Mr. Derek and the waitress came back. We left the ostrich sizzling and steaming like a Christmas turkey.

She was done to a turn.

Now we were on a real rampage, charging through the antiseptic corridors of Transmission House.

No one stopped us. It was Christmas Eve. Parties were going on in the building now, in different offices and rooms. You could hear the raucous shouts, the music, the clinking of bottles, and laughter. We shot past the open door of a news-room and got a glimpse of a very famous newsreader. In the middle of a cheering crowd, she was laughing and photo-copying her bum.

Tolstoy knew where we were going. He was calling the shots now. I couldn't have stopped him even if I'd tried.

We hurtled down a staircase into what seemed like the basement.

"Studio Nine." Tolstoy wheezed. "In the bowels of the earth."

We'd come to a door with a sign lit up in red above it.

"It used to be where we recorded my show, all those years ago."

"What's going on in there now?" I asked, but he was pushing the door open and we were forging our way into the darkness and hush beyond.

Immediately a short woman wearing headphones over masses of curly hair appeared before us. She was holding her clipboard. "You can't come in here," she stage-whispered. "They're recording *The Tootles Show*."

"The Tootles! Pah!" Tolstoy screamed, and dived at her face, whipping his wings about savagely.

The woman in the headphones squealed and fell back, tangled up in the cables that snaked across the studio floor.

We were in!

On a small, brightly lit set, the Tootles were in action. They were a family of kind of sock puppets who lived in a cartoony house with their grown-up friend, Simon. They sang songs and talked about rubbish. It was a show for little kids really. Even they would have to be out of their minds to watch it.

The Tootles' friend, Simon, was wearing red dungarees and he had a sock puppet on either hand, making them talk. He was facing a couple of really huge cameras and they were all taking it dead seriously. I had only a few seconds to absorb all of this before Tolstoy dragged me into their midst.

"What's going on?" shouted Simon the puppet master, as we leaped onto their brightly colored set. He looked furious at being interrupted. He glared at me and then at Tolstoy, who was being his most rabid and fierce.

"Tootle," said the sock puppet on Simon's left hand.

"Tootle tootle," said the one on his right.

That's all they could ever say. They were the Tootles.

"Bollocks!" roared Tolstoy. "Bollocks bollocks bollocks!"

Then he darted forward through the air. There was a flash of glistening yellow bat teeth and the next thing any of us knew, he'd clamped his jaws around the head of the Tootle nearest us.

"Owww-ww!" howled Simon.

"Tootle!" shrieked the other Tootle.

Tolstoy held on grimly, until he'd yanked the whole puppet off Simon's hand. Then he spat it on the floor, lifeless.

Simon stared at it, dumbfounded.

"That's what you get for broadcasting a shite show from the studio that used to be mine!" Tolstoy ranted. Then he flapped his wings powerfully and it was like he was flying and carrying me with him. We whirled around, back off the set in the middle of Studio Nine, and we were running away.

Tolstoy was quaking with malicious laughter.

"After them!" a voice was shouting through the sound system. "Don't let them get away!"

We were on a roll, though. There was no catching us.

We were too nimble and quick and we had the element of shock and horror on our side.

We pelted into a lift and Tolstoy was jabbing at the buttons with his snout, still laughing.

"Did you see that soft bastard's face when I scragged his sock puppet? Hahahahahaha!"

"Where now?" I asked breathlessly.

On the floor of Studio Six the special effects men were fiddling with the complicated miniature set for *Galaxy Patrol*. It was a space station with loads of intricate parts, and spaceships lying around.

We managed to get in and made one mad dash across the set, kicking at and trampling on all the special effects. "Rubbish!" Tolstoy was shouting. "It's just made out of washing-up bottles and cornflakes packets!"

Before we were chased off we even nicked a couple of tiny special-effects bombs and detonators. These came in useful when we visited Studio Two, where Jimmy the giraffe and his animal chums were rehearsing a song about what a lovely place the whole world would be, if people could only get along in peace and harmony. We lobbed a couple of *Galaxy Patrol* space grenades into their midst and that got them screaming.

"There are puppet shows everywhere!" I said as we ran away from the scenes of carnage in Studio Two.

"Too many," Tolstoy agreed. "Far too many of these useless freaks. They're far too popular. There's only one really good puppet and that's me! Tolstoy's the best puppet there ever was!"

Then we crashed into Studio One.

We were getting quite good at gate-crashing by now.

But this was the biggest studio of all. It had banks of seats for the live audience and these were all filled with studio guests and many famous faces, human and puppet. They were turning to look, startled, as Tolstoy and I came in.

In the center of the room, *The Barry Lurcher Show* was broadcasting live. Under the shadow of a large Christmas tree, on a gorgeous set made up to look like the drawing room of Barry's palatial mansion, the guests on his show were sitting. They were all looking horrified at the sight of Tolstoy and me.

There was a big blown-up picture of Nixon the penguin behind them. Barry was sitting there with my mam, Marjorie Staynes and Josephine the sea horse. All of their mouths were round Os of shock.

No one said anything as we approached. All of the cameras swung round to face us.

Tolstoy grinned into them as we stepped onto the set.

There was no applause.

Tolstoy flapped his tattered wings.

"Thank you, thank you, friends in the studio and friends at home! Here's a nice surprise for each and every one of you. I am back! Tolstoy, the greatest longest-eared bat in this whole rubbishy world, is back on your TV screens at last!"

Twenty-two

I was about to say that what happened next in Studio One was that all hell broke loose. But it was later in the story that that happened. This was a bit less chaotic, but it was noisy nonetheless.

I stood there, the center of attention, under all the spotlights, with everyone staring in horror at me and Tolstoy. The bat had run out of things to say and he was just preening himself in the full glare of the cameras.

I remember wondering if Dad would be watching this from his bed in the Light Entertainment Sanatorium and what he would think of it.

But then the next thing I knew, Barry had taken a flying leap and rugby-tackled me.

His own brother!

He really was a traitor, just like Dad always said.

Everyone in the audience was on their feet. They'd realized at last that this wasn't part of the "Tribute to Nixon" show. I'd fallen heavily and Tolstoy was flopping about, furious, on the rough carpet. Barry was clinging on and shouting at me, and so was Mam, who'd come hurrying over and was in tears.

Tolstoy snarled. I knew he wasn't about to let go of his moment of glory so easily. He rose up and struggled, lashing out at everyone with his claws and wings. He even scratched me down my arms and, next thing we all knew, he had flung himself on the only other puppet present on the set with a great shout of jubilation.

Josephine was taken completely by surprise. She squawked horribly, once, as Tolstoy snapped her up in his slavering jaws and proceeded to shake the life out of her. The water in her bucket was soon whipped up into a froth.

Marjorie was screaming, Mam was screaming and Barry was bellowing at the top of his voice. Somewhere, over the roar of the studio audience, the director was shouting instructions to go to an advert break, or to run the footage of the penguin funeral again.

I remember seeing the sea horse's stitching burst open and stuffing going everywhere, and then the Christmas tree was toppling over.

It fell on all of us, with a great tinkling, glittering crash, and I was knocked unconscious.

"Oh, Jason, how could you?" were the first words I heard when I woke up.

It was Mam. She was perched by my bedside in the green-and-scarlet outfit she'd chosen to wear on the show. Her hair looked a state and she had a cut above one eye. She was sobbing. "How *could* you?"

I was just staring back at her.

What had I done? I couldn't quite believe that any of it was true.

My throat felt parched. "W-where's Tolstoy?"

"*Him?*" Mam spat. "That thing?"

"Where is he?" Even I was alarmed at the desperation in my voice.

"My own son, a murderer of puppets," Mam said, sounding desolate. "I don't know what your father's going to say. And poor Marjorie! She's gone into a coma at the shock of losing Josephine. They've got her in this same hospital. I shall have to go and visit her after I've seen to you. You've ruined everything, Jason! Barry's show was a shambles! They had to take it off the air because of what you and that furry maniac did!"

Mam burst into tears again and I couldn't make out the rest of what she was saying.

"Is that where I am, then, hospital?" I asked.

"The police are coming to talk to you," she said at last. "About all of your activities tonight."

It was a bit hazy in my mind. I remembered being in a few different TV studios. I remembered having what had seemed at the time like the time of my life. I remember running about and laughing my head off and . . . taking revenge.

"Did I kill many puppets?"

"Loads," she said. "Loads of them. They're already calling it the 'Christmas Eve Massacre.'"

I lifted up my arm and stared at it. It looked oddly naked without Tolstoy there. Where had he gone?

"I told you I didn't want to be a puppeteer, Mam."

She was staring at me like I was some kind of monster.

"He's too strong for me, Mam. Tolstoy. He takes me over. Makes me do things . . ."

Mam looked incredulous. She got up and walked across the hospital room. Then she rummaged in my sports bag, which was resting on a chair. Out came Tolstoy like a lifeless rag and she waved him in my face.

"This?" she shouted. "This ratty bit of old fur? Possesses you, does he? Makes you do bad things? Pah!"

"It's true, Mam," I said, flinching away from the bat as she shook him. His empty eyes were goggling at me.

"That's rubbish, Jason. That's just the superstitious way all the puppeteers talk. But it isn't true. Not in the real world . . ."

"It is! It is!"

We were shouting at each other by now.

She sighed heavily and I fell quiet. She looked much older somehow. The bit of red tinsel in her hair made me feel sad all of a sudden. My mam looked like a very disappointed woman.

"There's no talking to you when you're like this," she said, looking away from me. "There's too much of your father in you."

"Mam . . ."

"Don't, Jason. I don't want to talk to you just now."

She dropped Tolstoy on the floor, beside my bed. His wings made a leathery slap on the linoleum. "I'm going to sit with poor Marjorie," she said. "I'm going to keep a vigil by her bedside, the poor old thing. You've broken her heart tonight, Jason. I hope you know that."

I watched my mam as she walked to the door.

She looked back and her eyes were glistening. "All of the Tootles are traumatized as well," she said. "I hope you can live with yourself after this, son."

She opened the door and almost collided with Lisa Turmoil, who was breathless and flustered.

"Is he all right?" I heard Lisa say. My heart rate had gone up at the sight of her.

"Him?" Mam snorted. "He's fine. But just about as crackers as his dad. Reckons the bat made him do it."

"Can I see him?" Lisa asked.

Mam shrugged and, without a backward glance, left me alone with Lisa. I heard Mam's shoes clipping away down the corridor.

Lisa slipped into my room.

"She thinks I'm a monster," I said. "My own mam. I think she's disowned me."

Lisa looked down at me, all businesslike. She had her

sleeves rolled up and had her hands on her hips. Her hair was a mess, but she looked very pretty.

"Your mam won't disown you. Not after we've proved your innocence and sorted everything out."

"What do you mean?" I asked. "It's hopeless. Everyone saw what I did. . . ."

"Moping around in hospital isn't going to help you," she announced. "You only banged your head a bit. Come on. You're getting up."

"The police are coming to question me!"

"Then we'll escape."

"Escape!"

She yanked back my blankets and made me get up. "You're not to blame, Jason. It was all down to that creature. That Tolstoy."

"You believe me?" As I stepped out of my bed and my feet hit the cold linoleum, my toes brushed the fur of the dropped bat's body and I pulled them away automatically.

"Of course," Lisa said. "I've been around puppets long enough to know what goes on. And you've been under the control of a very nasty piece of work indeed. Now, get dressed quickly, Jason, and pop Tolstoy in this bag. I'll watch the door."

I couldn't get dressed with her standing there. Even in

the direness of the situation, I was still embarrassed.

"I won't look," she said, grinning, and went to stand by the door. "Then I'll smuggle you and Tolstoy out. Somehow."

"But . . . ," I said, grabbing my sports bag. "Where are we going?"

She looked at me very seriously. "To find out some answers. We're going to ask your dad. We're going to the showbiz asylum!"

Twenty-three

We went driving through the night in Lisa Turmoil's Mini. It was snowing heavily as we made our escape and Lisa had to concentrate hard, pressing her nose almost up against the windshield to see where we were going. The windshield wipers had no sooner cleared the falling snow away before more was covering the glass.

I sat in the passenger seat and shivered. I didn't know whether that was out of fear or excitement. We were on the run! From the police and Barry and even my mam. And we were running towards my dad. I could hardly credit it. And what's more, it was Christmas night and I'd been unconscious for most of it. I'd missed everything.

Here I was with this woman I fancied. I'd tried to go off her because she thought I was a kid. I'd tried to push her out of my mind . . . and that's when Tolstoy had taken over completely. But now Lisa was with me. She was risking everything to be with me.

I asked Lisa if the whole country was talking about the boy and the bat who had ruined Barry's Christmas Eve show. She turned to give me a funny smile.

"A certain number of eyebrows were raised," she said. "But actually it made quite good TV. You'd be surprised. People seemed to like seeing Barry made a fool of. He's not that popular."

"Really?" I had to pretend to be surprised. "Dad was always less popular than Tolstoy too."

"It's often the way," Lisa sighed. "The puppet takes over the puppeteer."

Now we were on the motorway. It was mostly empty. One of those nights when the radio tells you not to venture out in the weather unless your journey is strictly necessary. Well, ours was.

Lisa seemed to know exactly where we were going. "It isn't too far," she said. "Just outside the city. Soon be there."

By now I was gritting my teeth. Tolstoy was trying to talk

to me. I had been trying to put up a kind of defense against all his insidious whispers, but it wasn't much of one. My sports bag was on the Mini's backseat. I was imagining Tolstoy's claws scraping at the insides, teasing at the zipper. What if he came springing out?

But that was stupid. He wasn't able to move of his own accord. Course he wasn't.

"I don't want to hurt you," I said to Lisa. I looked at her.

"What?" She looked a bit startled.

"If Tolstoy possesses me again, I don't want you getting hurt."

She shook her head. "Puppets can't hurt people. Only other puppets."

I shrugged. "You believe me, don't you, Lisa?"

"Yes," she said. "I think so." She looked at me. "No, I know so. I know you wouldn't have done any of this without Tolstoy making you do it."

Tolstoy had gone quiet now. I knew he was lying in that bag, simmering with rage. There wasn't anything he could do.

"I should never have gone to him," I said. "I went up to the attic and let him out. He was calling to me."

"I've read about things like this," said Lisa. "Puppets can be very frightening creatures. People don't realize. You hear some very funny stories when you're a hairstylist."

I wanted to thank her for believing me. But the words just wouldn't come. I was still shy of her. I realized I was worn out.

I must have drifted into sleep because the next thing I knew we were moving slowly, up a dark lane. The snow was heavier here and had drifted into peculiar, whipped-up shapes. The black branches of trees hung down over us as the car's headlights probed into the darkness. We were inching along up a driveway.

"Are we here?"

Lisa nodded tersely. "I'm taking us in the back way, I think."

"Were we followed?"

"I don't think so." She was biting her lip like she wasn't sure.

At least the police couldn't do me for murder. We hadn't hurt any actual people. But I still didn't want to be caught.

I was wondering what I was going to say to my dad when we found him. What state he was going to be in.

The car slid by these weird, ghost-like shapes carved into the snow. Maybe the wind had made them, or maybe the inmates of the sanatorium came out to play and made snowmen during the day. The weirdest kind of snowmen in the world.

We slowed to a halt in the deep snow of a car park round the back.

"Most of the staff will be gone," Lisa said. "It should be easy enough getting in." She had a bag of tools with her. They were mostly hairstyling tools, but she had a crowbar with her too.

The asylum was a tall, Gothic monstrosity. It had towers and turrets sticking out everywhere. It looked a bit broken down and grotesque really. The sort of place you'd have to be out of your mind to visit. Lisa was being so determined and

helpful, though, I didn't dare look reluctant to get out of the Mini and follow her up to the big house.

You could see from here that the middle of the building had a great glass dome. It was all lit up green and you could hear thudding music going on within.

"It sounds like they're having a party inside," I said.

"It's Christmas after all," said Lisa. "Even showbiz maniacs have Christmas."

She had found a little door in a frozen, mildewed wall. "Looks like an old servants' entrance," she said and grimly set to work with her crowbar. It didn't have much effect on the frozen, rotten wood. Then, struck by inspiration, she fished around for hairclips in her bag and managed to pick the lock.

"I've all sorts of hidden talents," she said, grinning, as the old door creaked open.

Now we could hear the music quite clearly, echoing from inside the sanatorium. It was an old Christmas song. That one that goes, "I wish it could be Christmas every day."

Lisa took hold of my hand. "We might see some things inside that aren't very pleasant," she warned.

I gulped and realized I was carrying my sports bag in my other hand. Why couldn't I leave him behind? Would I never be free of him?

Lisa dragged me into a freezing, pitch-dark corridor.

It was obvious where the source of the noise was—a door at the end of this passageway. It must lead into the heart of the building.

"I'd have thought they'd have them all locked up and strapped down for the night . . . ," said Lisa worriedly.

But that wasn't how things were in the showbiz asylum at Christmas.

She gave the door at the end of the hall a firm shove and we walked through, into brilliant, blinding light.

Twenty-four

There was a show going on. It was obvious really, when you thought about it. Of course that's what the inmates would do, once they'd been left alone by the staff of the asylum and it was Christmas. They would put on one big spectacular show for their own entertainment.

Lisa and I stood holding our breath.

They had made a vast stage in the central hall out of all the bits of furniture they could find. Beds and desks and wardrobes and chairs had been piled on top of one another into a tottering structure that didn't look very safe at all. All the lights were blazing and they had rigged others up from the rafters to glare down at the various performances taking place. Most of the lights were a horrible lurid green.

The music was thudding extremely loudly. That same song, over and over.

The showbiz maniacs were all performing busily and shouting to be heard above the din. No one was watching anyone else, they were all just getting on with their own shows, on different parts of the stage. Some were hanging off the very top, others were standing on the floor. Ancient pop stars who had gone off their rockers in the 1960s were crooning or belting out their respective songs. Mad quiz-show hosts were dressed in their sequined tuxedos and were shuffling question cards and yelling Big Money Questions at contestants who weren't even there. There was a boxing ring where elderly and crazy weather girls were wrestling, as special-effects men recreated various kinds of weather from above, clinging to scaffolding. They had made a blizzard out of torn-up copies of the *Radio Times*.

Lisa and I were clutching each other's hands firmly.

We walked around the perimeter of the room, taking in all the details of the Christmas spectacular. We saw a troupe of dancers in pink tights and legwarmers not even trying to keep in step with one another. Newsreaders were sitting at a line of desks, each outshouting the others. A few decrepit pup-peteers were chatting away with their badgers, jackals and bunnies. But Dad wasn't there. We scanned all the faces, but we couldn't see him.

As one particular magician scooted busily past, I tugged at his elbow and asked after my dad.

"Who?" His faced creased up.

"Frank Lurcher," I said. "He must be here."

"And who are you?" asked the magician. He had a

sweating face and a pack of cards that he was shuffling manically. "And pick a card, would you?"

"I'm his son," I said, and slid a card out of the pack.

"And you're locked up here, are you, as well?"

"No," I said, and showed him the card.

His eyes lit up at the sight of Lisa. "And who is the lovely lady?"

"I'm a hairstylist," she said. "Lisa Turmoil."

"Maybe I could saw you in half?"

"Not on your nelly, chum," she told him. But then the sweating magician was calling out to the others. "Normal people! We've got normal people here! From outside! An audience!"

All of a sudden, the showbiz mad people stopped what they were doing. The dancers stopped high-kicking, the puppets fell quiet. The music died on the air.

Everyone was looking at us.

"Uh-oh," said Lisa. She dug me in the ribs. "I don't think we should have drawn attention to ourselves."

"Audience . . . ," some of the loonies were muttering. "Our audience . . ."

They were climbing down off their makeshift stages and the scaffolding. They were shuffling towards us with arms outstretched: singers and drag acts and fire-eaters. They were moving like zombies.

"Watch us . . . applaud us . . . give us marks out of ten . . ."

"When I say run," Lisa whispered, "turn round and . . ."

I didn't need telling twice.

"Run!" she screamed, just as the magician's hand tried to grab hold of her.

We both whirled around, ready to sprint.

And we stopped in our tracks.

My dad was standing in the doorway.

He was in a quilted red dressing gown and he was puffing at a cigarette holder. "Jason, Lisa." He smiled. "How lovely of you both to come to our little show."

"Dad?" I said. He looked better than he had in years. He'd even dyed his few hairs back to jet-black. It was like he had regained all of his celebrity status.

"But whatever possessed you," he purred, "to come out all this way to see me?"

"Tolstoy," I burst out. "Tolstoy possessed me!"

"Ah," said Dad. Then he barked at the assorted showbiz maniacs, "What are you all listening in for? Go back to your entertaining, at once!"

They did as they were told.

Dad ruled the school! I was amazed. Now he was leading us into another dark corridor.

"That terrible Tolstoy," he chuckled. "Whatever has he been up to now?"

Twenty-five

Our conversation in Dad's room was punctuated by crashes and bangs from the main hall, as the inmates became ever more enthusiastic in their exertions. From the muffled music and the shouting, it seemed that they were getting carried away.

Dad's room was as luxurious as any room in Barry's house. He had tall gilded mirrors with flashing lightbulbs all around and a golden high-backed chair, on which he settled himself before talking to us.

We were shocked. Somehow we'd both expected to find him still in his mucky straitjacket and moaning in despair.

"Dad!" I said. "How come you're, like, king of the loonies?"

He smiled and gave a hollow laugh. "Because I'm famous here, Jason!"

"You, famous?" I said tactlessly.

"Tell me," he said, "who did you recognize out there in the main hall?"

"Um . . . no one."

"Exactly!" He smiled. "I'm the most famous madman any of those madmen have ever seen in their lives. They're honored by my presence. They still remember me. Even if no one else does."

"Wow," said Lisa. "So you're happy here, Mr. Lurcher?"

He nodded beatifically. "Happier than I've been for years. And I don't even have to put on any puppet shows."

I flinched at that word, "puppet."

Dad looked at me sharply. His beaky nose was twitching. "He's here, isn't he?"

I played for time. "Who, Dad?"

"You know who I mean. He's here. He's in your bag. The one you're hiding behind your back. I can sense him. Close by." Suddenly Dad looked a whole lot less composed. His dyed-black eyebrows were beetling up his forehead. His hands were grasping up like claws.

"Yes," I admitted. "We brought him with us. But I daren't let him out of the bag."

Dad nodded. Then smiled. "Well, never mind. It's probably best that I don't see him again. I haven't missed him." He licked his thin lips.

"He's caused a lot of bother, Dad," I said.

"Heh heh. The tyke."

"It's true," Lisa put in. "He's ruined a few lives these past couple of days."

"He ruined all of my life!" Dad protested. "My life wasn't my own when that . . . that bat was around."

"Well," she said, "now he's moved on to Jason."

Dad raised a quizzical eyebrow at me. "What's this? Have you been trying to fill your old dad's shoes?" Then his face darkened abruptly. "The puppet murders . . . you mean . . ."

I nodded, shamefaced. "I think . . . I think it was me, Dad. Nixon and Toby and all the rest. It was all down to me." I hung my head and Lisa patted my shoulder in support. "But I wasn't in my right mind!"

Dad barked with laughter. "Nobody is, with a puppet like Tolstoy on the end of their arm." Now he was looking hungrily again at my sports bag. "If I could just take another look at him . . . for old time's sake. Just a little look . . . I won't bring him to life. . . ."

I could hear Tolstoy's voice in my head. "I wouldn't come to life for that old devil now anyway. He has to live without me. I'm not his anymore."

I shook my head. "No, Dad. He's too strong for me. I don't want to do any more damage. . . ."

Dad nodded testily. Then Lisa spoke up again.

"Mr. Lurcher, we've come here for some answers."

"Answers, is it, young woman?" Dad said querulously.

Tolstoy was rasping in my ear, "You won't like any of the answers you get, you know. Don't go asking too many questions, Jason. They won't make you happy. . . ."

"Shut up!" I said aloud.

"Take me out," Tolstoy went on. "I'll make you famous and rich. . . . You can have anything you desire. . . ."

"Shut up!" I yelled.

Lisa and Dad were looking at me strangely.

"Hmm," said Dad, recognizing all the signs. "I was a fool that day. We should have bought you your own puppet straight away. Something sweet-natured. Something . . . that wasn't evil."

"You should have!" agreed Lisa. "And you should have burned Tolstoy twenty years ago!"

Dad looked aghast. "Burned him! I couldn't have done that! He's real. As real as any of us."

"But why is he evil, Mr. Lurcher?" Lisa asked.

Dad hung his head.

"Yes," Tolstoy said. "Why am I so evil? I bet he doesn't tell you. . . ."

But Dad did tell us. He looked up and started his story.

"It goes back to when I was starting out as a puppeteer. Before Barry was born. I was a young man then and I hadn't been on the telly even once. And I . . . I made a pact with the devil."

I was shocked. "The devil!"

Lisa gripped my shoulder.

"Hahahahahahaha!" Tolstoy was going.

208

"I bought Tolstoy from a very old shop. I'd been told about this place . . . just whispers, rumors. An old shop off the beaten track, run by an extremely old puppeteer. He had every kind of puppet you could think of, all of them unique. And, being the kind of foolhardy and inquisitive young man who always wound up in hot water, I followed my nose to this place. I was determined to find my own puppet. The one that was right just for me."

"And you found . . . him?"

"He certainly did!" Tolstoy laughed.

"The old man in the puppet shop was about two hundred years old if he was a day. His shop was filled with dust and cobwebs, like no one ever went there. Like he'd been waiting for me for decades. And I go strolling in, easy as you like. And all of these faces were gazing down at me from shelves that went up to the ceiling. All kinds of faces and heads with these blank, staring eyes. Each one was beseeching me. They all wanted choosing and taking out into the world."

Dad's voice had gone quieter as he thought himself back. Lisa and I were listening hard.

"The old puppet master behind the wooden counter explained to me the importance of making the right choice. He said that the right puppet waits for you. Exactly the right puppet for the person you are. That face and those blank eyes are waiting on a shelf for you somewhere and you have to come along and recognize that spark there between you. You can't get it wrong, or the magic, the unique magic, will never work.

"So I spent hours that afternoon checking through the shelves. Going up ladders and opening boxes and hunting through the storeroom. The old puppet master was very helpful. Too helpful. And I just knew somehow, deep down, that he was waiting there for me, somewhere. The right puppet. Tolstoy.

"And he was.

"He was a horrible-looking thing even then. Malevolent, ratty. A bit grimy. He'd need some cleaning up before I could work with him. But I knew at first sight that he was the right one. The only one. I knew that the magic would work."

"And how did the devil come in?" Lisa burst out.

Dad admonished her with a glance. "When I told the shopkeeper that I had made my choice he looked very downcast. Oh, I knew he was faking it, to get a higher price. But I was prepared to pay anything. I knew that Tolstoy the long-eared bat was my puppet. I knew he'd been lying in wait for me. But, "Oh, sir, please, young sir. Do not take my old bat away from me. Of all the puppets in my shop, please don't take that one! I beg of you, sir!"

"Well, that just made me want the bat all the more. You know how it is."

Tolstoy himself had fallen quiet by now. It was as if he was relishing the telling of the tale.

"I wouldn't heed the foolish old man's words. I assumed he was simply being greedy. With a young man's arrogance, I pushed the bat across the scratched wooden counter for wrapping up and I took out my wallet, fingering the stash of notes I'd folded away in there. I'd been saving for months. Playing my ukelele on the underground and in working-men's clubs."

"I didn't know you could play the ukelele, Dad."

"There are many things you don't know about me, Jason," he said darkly.

"Go on with the story," urged Lisa.

"The old man flustered and refused. 'No, no, I will not sell you Tolstoy,' he said, waving his hands in my face. 'I brought him out of the old country with me. He is too precious. He has seen too much . . .' Now I was laying the crisp green notes on the counter, one after another. The shopkeeper's eyes lit up. I knew he wasn't used to getting any customers at all. I knew he'd have to be near penniless. And, of course, greed got the better of him. 'But you must promise to look after him, sir,' he said. 'To be the best master a bat could ever have. I am

an old, old man and soon I will die. Soon all my puppets will be masterless. They will need good, decent homes and . . .'
'Yes, yes,' I said impatiently. I have always been an impatient and irritable person, even as a young man."

"So you got the puppet," said Lisa. "How does the devil come into this?"

Dad's expression was very strange. Crafty. Lit up. Satanic. He was right. There were many things I didn't know about him.

"The shop owner had another condition, besides my giving Tolstoy a good home," he said. "And that was that I learned to become a proper puppeteer. That I learned the secret, magic art in the correct manner. And that was when he told me he wasn't just some innocuous old man in a dusty shop, but really an emissary of the devil."

"And you believed him!" I gasped.

"I had to," Dad said. "I was very serious about becoming a puppet master. And soon I was under the old man's influence. And I was drawn into a coven of witches and warlocks out Shepherd's Bush way. We used to meet once a fortnight to burn a few candles, dance around, generally make merry and, if we were lucky, call up our friendly neighborhood demon. I felt like I had found my vocation in life."

Lisa and I looked at each other briefly, shocked.

"Anyway, after months of this kind of carrying-on and learning to speak without moving my lips and all the other important things a puppeteer needs to know, the old shopkeeper, who was himself a very powerful magician, said that I had to complete my training by going to the gateway."

"The gateway?" Lisa asked.

"It was a gateway to hell itself," said Dad. "Bang in the middle of a certain forest just north of where I lived. Just off the M-25 as it is now. Of course, the M-25 wasn't there back then."

"A gateway to hell?" I gasped.

"Yes," he said. "And it was well known, in all the old and secret books, that the devil himself would pop out of this gateway for a little chat or whatever if you really wanted him to. Well, I was quite keen."

"Keen!" cried Lisa.

Dad nodded. "I wanted success! I wanted everything! The devil seemed the simplest way. He always seemed to grant wishes to people in the old stories. And the ancient shopkeeper told me on his deathbed—he was right about not having long left—that I had to ask the devil a favor, just like in the stories."

"It's always at a terrible price," said Lisa.

"Well, as I say, I was an impatient young man." Dad

coughed. "I never actually got to the end of the old stories. I just assumed they always ended well."

"They don't!" Lisa said.

"I know that now," he said sharply. "I was a fool, a fool to ask for what the shopkeeper told me to . . ." He started crying, all of a sudden. It was alarming to see.

"Did the devil come to you?"

Dad nodded gravely. "And he brought Tolstoy to life."

I caught my breath. "What?"

Dad pointed at the sports bag, which I had dropped on the floor. "That puppet is the puppet of Satan himself."

We all stared at the bag.

Faint laughter came bubbling up from within.

We could all hear it.

Twenty-six

We never went to church or anything like that, but I was still a bit shocked. My own dad! A devil worshiper! I told you though, didn't I? He's a bit evil. All I meant then was that he was grumpy sometimes. Now he was really telling me that he'd sold his soul to Beelzebub!

"I was very young," he sighed. "It was years ago now. Probably the devil's gone and forgotten all about it. He must buy loads of the things."

Lisa shook her head solemnly. "He always remembers. It happened to my Aunty Pat."

"Oh," said Dad.

"What was the devil like?" I asked.

"Quite nice really," Dad said. "Polite, you know. It wasn't all that dramatic, truth be told. I just went out to the woods in the middle of the night. In all the snow. Christmas night, in fact! Why, the same night as tonight! Forty years ago! To the day!"

"Spooky coincidence," said Lisa.

"Maybe *not* a coincidence." Dad frowned. "Anyway, up he pops from this gaping hole in the ground. The gateway to hell, that was, and it wasn't that spectacular. Nice suit on. A

bunch of forms to fill in. Well, you have to fill in forms for everything, don't you? And the next thing I knew . . . Tolstoy had this life of his own. More than the other puppets."

"The best puppet in all the world!" came the bat's muffled voice from my bag. "The greatest bat of all time!"

"But he could only live when I was there," Dad said. "There was that bond between us. And now it's between you and him, Jason. I was wondering why I'd been feeling so much better just lately."

"You have to help Jason, Mr. Lurcher," said Lisa earnestly. "You have to help him get rid of Tolstoy."

"Get rid?" Dad looked perplexed.

"GET RID!" yelled Tolstoy.

"He's going to fight his way out of that bag," said Lisa worriedly.

"He won't hurt Jason," Dad said. "Jason's his best pal in the whole world."

"Dad," I said, "how do I send him away?"

Dad's face looked old and very serious. He looked more human than I'd ever seen him. He even looked like he thought something of me. "Is that what you want, Jason? To be rid of him?"

I nodded.

"But he's your friend for life," Dad said. "He's guaranteed always to be on your side. And he'll never leave your side, ever. You'll never be lonely. He might even make you famous and rich. . . ."

"But he makes me do bad things!"

Dad nodded wisely. "I fell out with him for just that reason. He was taking too much control. My life wasn't my own. He wanted me to kill Barry's penguin even then."

"So you put him in the attic . . ."

"And I thought he'd never come down again."

"What do we do, Dad?"

Dad said, "It's quite simple. We go back to the gateway. Back to the forest. On the very anniversary of his becoming, we take him back. And we make another bargain with the devil."

Lisa and I both gulped.

Dad grinned. "Don't worry. I'll be coming with you. But

first . . . you've got to get me out of here. Out of the asylum. It's very nice and everything, but everyone's a bit mad."

It was at this point that a worse hullabaloo started up in the main hall.

We could hear it very clearly. The maniacs were chanting, "Audience! Real people! Audience!" all over again, in a very alarming and excitable manner.

"Hello," said Dad, listening thoughtfully as he stood up from his golden chair. "I think we might have company. . . ." We left Dad's room and rushed back to the main hall, where all the noise was coming from. Dad was right. Other people had come in besides us, and they were disturbing the inmates' Christmas night revels. Not that the inmates were upset. They seemed delighted. They were all shouting out, "More audience! More real people!" And then they started doing their acts again, faster, louder, even more enthusiastically. Jugglers threw things higher, fire-eaters blew flames out with extra vigor and magicians sawed into maniac assistants with gusto. The lights were flashing more busily, as if the mad stagehands wanted to show off as well.

"Oh, no," moaned Lisa, when she saw what was going on. She stood behind me, clutching my shoulders.

"They've caught up with you," my dad said mildly.

I'd never heard him say anything mildly in my life. I

couldn't get used to this new, calm, gentle Dad who wore padded purple dressing gowns and went on like he was happier in himself. It just wasn't like him.

Meanwhile I was holding my sports bag up to my chest, muffling the thumps and all the thrashing about that were going on inside it. We had more pressing concerns now than Tolstoy's trying to escape.

Barry's production company had caught up with us. He was there, directing his cameramen, and they were shooting the documentary again. They were filming every scrap of what was going on in the showbiz asylum. They just wouldn't let any opportunity go by.

Worst of all, though, was that Mam was there.

She had got herself a new job. She was a presenter, right in front of the camera. She was describing to the viewers at home just what was going on, in case they couldn't figure it out for themselves. She was in a strapless blue frock and she looked very at home in her new role. She was talking into a microphone and the peering lens of the camera as if that was the most natural thing in the world. She was putting on a posher voice too.

"Poor Eileen," Dad murmured. "She always loved the telly. I never let her watch it much, did I? That was rather cruel of me. Look at how she's enjoying herself, being filmed. She's in her element."

I stared at him.

"I held her back," Dad said. "That woman is made for television."

"They're filming the sanatorium!" I said. "They've come following us! They're going to make you into a laughingstock again, Dad!"

But he only shrugged. "That's what I always was, Jason. I used to sit there talking to a long-eared bat. I was the butt of his jokes. I wanted people to laugh at me. What's so different now?"

"We have to get away," Lisa said decisively, squeezing my shoulders. "Otherwise they'll lead the police here and you'll have questions to answer . . ."

I was watching my Mam attempting to interview one of the mad people. "How long have you been living here?" she asked brightly. It was the man with the pack of cards. He didn't understand her question. He just wanted her to pick a card, any card.

It was Barry who saw us and shouted. He thrust his arm out, pointing above the heads of the attention-seeking mob. His favorite skinny cameraman swung round to get us on film. "Don't make any sudden moves," I heard Barry warn his crew as they struggled towards us. "That kid is dangerous."

The cheek of it! "Did you hear that?" I asked Lisa.

"I think we should just get out to the Mini," Lisa said, starting to back away. She knew she'd already blown her job as hairstylist to the stars.

Tolstoy was almost ripping my sports bag apart from the inside.

"Jason!" Mam was shouting. "I want to interview you!"

It was my dad who took hold of my arm and dragged me out of the main hall. He knew the best way to the car park, where the snow was still coming down. We left with the cries of the inmates ringing in our ears as they begged their audience to stay and watch them . . .

In the Mini, as Lisa gunned the engine and set the windshield wipers going, Dad told me, "Keep a tight hold, Jason, and don't let that bat out of the bag. We've got an hour or so to drive. I know the way. Keep a tight grip on Tolstoy. Then, when we get there, I'll find us the gateway to hell. I'm sure I can. And we can send him back to where he came from. . . ."

Twenty-seven

Tolstoy must have known he was beaten—or on his way to a really good beating—because he kept coming into my head and whispering promises. All the way round the M-25, through the middle of that blizzardy night, Tolstoy was going on and on about what the future could be if only we didn't send him back to hell.

Dad was sitting in the passenger seat now, so he could give directions to Lisa. The only trouble was, his memory had grown a little vague in the forty years since he'd been out to this mysterious forest.

"What are we going to do?" shouted Lisa, exasperated. "Drive round and round the M-25 all night till it comes back to you?" She was hunched over the steering wheel, her voice sounding raw with frustration.

No one had pointed out that Dad had left the asylum wearing his dressing gown and silk pajamas. Maybe because he looked so comfortable in them.

Lisa and Dad's getting tetchy with each other—"Don't you talk to me like that, young lady!"—fell into the background of my thoughts. Tolstoy was saying things.

"We could host a great big talent show together. We

could get ordinary people on the telly and make them think they're big stars. And then we would have to judge them and we could tell them they were just awful! We could make them cry! It would be really funny!"

I was determined not to listen.

"When we were really huge stars on TV, then we could go on and make films together. I bet we'd be huge box-office smashes. And I don't mean crappy cutesy films like puppets usually make. I mean proper movies, action movies, with guns and bank robberies and car chases and everything."

"I'm not listening, Tolstoy," I whispered at my sports bag.

"Ah, but you're talking to me again," he snickered. "That's a start, at least. I mean it, Jason, I've got the talent and the power to make us the biggest human–puppet double act the world has ever seen. Don't you want to make anything of your life, eh? Will you be content just to be a nobody?"

I sighed. "No one will watch us, Tolstoy. We couldn't be stars. We're already wanted criminals."

"Excellent! That's a brilliant start!"

"And no one will watch you, after you killed poor Josephine the sea horse live on Christmas Eve. . . ."

"Are you kidding?" he crowed. "Everyone's been waiting for years for that to happen. That snooty-nosed fish thing should have been scragged ages ago. They'll thank me!"

Dad had turned in his seat and was peering at me from under his bushy eyebrows. "Were you saying something, Jason?"

"No, I . . ."

Dad's face darkened. "You were talking to *him* again, weren't you?"

It was useless to argue.

"Well, don't," Dad went on. "It's too dangerous."

Lisa, who was peering into the rear-view mirror, suddenly swore. "Company," she said.

Through the swarming snow behind us it was hard to pick out the silver van. "Barry's lot," I said.

"Plus your mam," added Dad. "That woman's the crazy one! What are they going to do? Follow us all the way to the gateway to hell and ask for an interview with the devil himself?"

Lisa said, "They don't know where we're going or what we're planning to do."

"Then it'll come as a nice surprise to them," Dad replied with relish. "And this is our turn-off! Turn! Turn! Don't signal! Try to throw them off our scent!" He was grabbing at the steering wheel, making Lisa cry out. The car veered and rocked wildly and I was thrown about from side to side on the backseat.

Then we were whizzing round a roundabout much too fast and slipping into a dark, unlit side road. Into the countryside.

"This is it!" Dad was shouting. "I remember now!"

I wound down my window and stuck my head out into the roaring blizzard. "They're still after us!"

The silver van was glowing through the snow like some furious monster. In the yellow of its cab I could see Barry, Mam and the cameraman, recording every second of the chase. I waved to them, trying to make them go back. They took no notice. The snow was stinging at my face.

"Faster! Faster!" Dad was screaming now. "Drive faster, Lisa Turmoil!"

Lisa was really putting her foot down. I looked ahead. I could just about pick out the looming shapes of the treetops ahead. We'd reached it. This was the forest that Dad had talked about.

"Faster, you silly girl!" he yelled.

Before I knew it I had my sports bag open.

I had my hand in among the tattered fur of Tolstoy's body. His wings were unfolding. They started beating and flapping and slashing their way out of the bag, into the confined space of Lisa's Mini.

"Free!" he rasped. "I'm . . . free!"

The car was just starting to slow down as the road

beneath us became frozen dirt track. We were entering the woods, vibrating like crazy. Both Lisa and Dad were startled by the outburst from the backseat. They didn't even have time to react.

"Free!" Tolstoy squawked.

I put all of my weight on the handle and flung open the door. While the car was still moving on the rutted road, the two of us went tumbling out into the snow. . . .

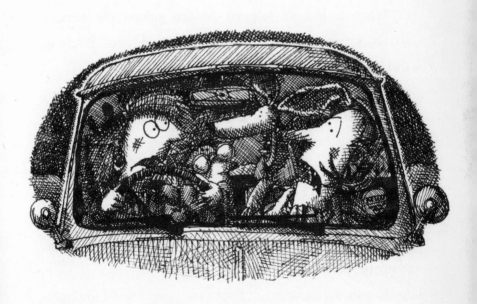

Twenty-eight

Over and over through the thick and frozen drifts.

The world had turned stark black and white: the flat black of the sky and the woods, and the searing brilliance of the snow as we cartwheeled through it, sending great flurries and plumes into the air.

We were falling down into a ditch, through the underbrush, almost burying ourselves in the drifts as we tried to escape.

When at last we stopped, hidden among the trees, I started brushing snow off Tolstoy's fur. He was coughing and shaking himself. We paused for a moment.

Shouting. Cries. Up where we'd left the others in the Mini.

Dad and Lisa had come running in search of us. They were calling out. The van must have pulled to a halt too. Other voices were joining them.

They wouldn't find us right away. We had time to take the advantage. My shoulder had been banged, and both knees, as I found when I tried to run. It felt like I'd twisted the wrist of my puppet hand, too.

Tolstoy was snarling, "You took your time! I thought you'd betrayed me. Now where are we? Middle of frigging nowhere, that's where!"

I couldn't reply. I was ducking down, weaving between trees, listening to the shouts from behind as the others hunted for us.

Dad was yelling at Mam, "Can't you stop them filming us? This is your own son we've lost here!"

"What?" she yelled back at him. "I know who he is! You don't have to remind me! And who started all this business in the first place? Who's the one really to blame?"

"Oh, that'll be me, will it?"

"Stop it, both of you!" Barry bellowed.

"Right," Tolstoy told me. "While they're fighting. Let's make a run for it. Through the trees. Come on!"

I had no choice. Once again, when Tolstoy announced his idea, all I could do was get up, out of the snow and follow him. On shaking, aching legs, we plunged into the forest, through the frozen black trunks of the trees.

Lisa's voice rose out of the kerfuffle behind us. "There they are! Look! They're getting away!"

All their arguments stopped at once.

"Run!" Tolstoy howled into my ear.

I stole one backward glance. I saw Lisa leading the way, flinging herself into the snow-drifted ditch we'd fallen into. She was followed by the less nimble figure of my dad, startling in his scarlet dressing gown. Behind them came a jumble

of TV people with their lights and cameras and, among them,
full of determination, Barry and my mam.

"Run!" screamed Tolstoy again.

We were still a fair distance ahead of them.

But we didn't know where we were going.

The forest seemed like the biggest, densest, darkest forest
that the world had ever known. Anything could be living here.
Anything at all. We ploughed and shuffled on, through snow
that was up to my knees, soaking through my jeans and numb-
ing my legs. I don't know how long we ran like that, crashing
through frost-rimed branches with a terrible clatter.

Tolstoy lunged ahead, his wings flaring out, trying to go
faster than I could ever manage. My breathing was coming in
ragged bursts and my heart was pounding. We could hear the
calls and cries of everyone pursuing us, echoing weirdly under
the canopy of trees.

"They're catching us up!" Tolstoy shouted. There was
a note of despair in his voice now. "Why do they hate me
so much? Why have they *always* hated me so much? It's not
fair. All I want is just what any puppet wants. And your dad
locked me up in a box for twenty years. He hid me away
and forgot all about me! He wished I was dead and I might
as well have been. Now they all want to send me away—
forever! It's not fair, Jason!" He thrust his snout into my

face. "Tell me, Jason. Why do they hate me so much?"

I could hardly draw breath. I stopped in my tracks and had to lean against the harsh bark of a tree. I was stooped over, heart bursting, telling him, "I don't know, Tolstoy. I don't know. . . ." I was confused. At that moment I truly couldn't see how they could hate him. He was the greatest puppet in the world.

Then his snout jerked up and his green eyes dulled in fear. "They're here," he rasped.

Dad, Lisa, Barry, Mam and the others had caught up with us. They came staggering, panting, across the snow towards us.

"Jason, love . . . ," Mam was calling.

"Don't move," Dad barked. "Don't make a move. Let my son go!"

Barry was shouting at his technical people. "Don't miss a second of this! Not a second! Your jobs depend on this!"

"Keep back," Tolstoy growled.

They kept their distance. We were all trying to get our breath back. The snow was falling again, drifting and sifting through the treetops towering over us.

"Keep right back," said Tolstoy, in a voice thick with hatred and fear. "Don't you dare try to separate us. You can't. Not now. We're bonded, me and Jason! You can't tear us apart!"

Dad was the one who stepped forward, looking thoughtful. He seemed to glide on the churned-up snow in his vivid quilted dressing gown. "Have you asked Jason how he feels about that, hm? Have you asked if he wants to be bonded with a nasty-mouthed, foul-tempered, evil-minded wretch like you?" Dad smiled. Snowflakes were settling on his gleaming bald skull.

"Of course he wants to be with me," Tolstoy snapped. Though he sounded less sure of himself by now.

Dad laughed softly. "Tolstoy," he said sadly, "you are a very, very bad puppet."

I could feel the long-eared bat begin to quake with fear. I could feel it all the way up my arm.

"W-what are you going to do, Frank?" He was trying to make his voice sound braver.

From his dressing-gown pocket Dad produced something very like a magic wand. He waved it grandly in the air. "What am I going to do, Tolstoy?" He pulled a face. "Magic." He whooshed the wand about, through the snow. "For the last time in my life, I'm going to try a spot of black magic."

Mam screamed out at this. "No, Frank! You can't!"

Tersely he said, "Keep back, Eileen. I know what I'm doing. I think."

"He's right, Eileen," said Barry. "Keep over here."

"Be careful, Mr. Lurcher . . . ," said Lisa.

Tolstoy and I were just staring in horror at what Dad was doing.

Then he said the magic words. Words he had stored in his memory these past forty years. Words that came from ancient, mysterious, forbidden books.

He coughed. He raised his voice. He waved the gnarled old wand.

"Yzziw yzzi!
Ysub teg stel!"

There was a pause.

Then a huge grinding, crashing, rumbling, shrieking howl seemed to come from the very bowels of the earth.

The ground shook and snow dropped in heavy clumps off the branches as all the trees shook and their roots were dislodged.

A huge gash was opening up in the clean white snow between us. It ran in a zigzag as the earthquake reached its cataclysmic height.

Then all hell really did break loose.

Twenty-nine

At first it was dark. That dirty great hole Dad had made in the ground with his magic words was just dark and still.

Then there were flames.

All of us fell back a few steps in shock. Great spurting flames came spewing out of the pit. They were brighter than anything I'd ever seen before in my life and they looked nothing like real fire. Licking tongues of flame: orange and purple, green and gold. They were ferocious. They soared up into the freezing air, melting the snow back. There was an aggrieved sizzling from the ice as the flames went leaping.

Most of the others were lying down now, blown off their feet. They were staring and their faces had turned white. Oddly enough, I was closest to the flaming chasm and I was still standing up. Dad was too, his dressing gown buffeted by the heat's hellish blast.

Tolstoy was shouting harder than ever. He'd pulled his satin wings close into his body, for fear of their burning. He was crushing his head into my chest. He didn't dare look at the inferno before us.

"I call you!" Dad shouted above all of the noise. "I dare to call you forth! Once, forty human years ago, I called you and now I, Francis Lurcher, dare to call on you again!"

For a moment nothing happened. Just the wicked flames, crackling and licking at the very tops of the trees. I looked to Dad and saw he was scared.

He called again.

"We desire an audience with the Great One himself!"

In my arms, burying his snout in my coat, Tolstoy whimpered and wailed.

"Make him stop, Jason! Oh, make him stop!"

But then a huge voice echoed through the dark woods, and that stopped all our talk. It stopped each and every thought in our heads. Every limb on every tree trembled as that huge voice spoke.

It wasn't a deep voice. It was kind of . . . squeaky.

But it was still loud.

"Who dares to disturb my rest?"

We each watched Dad gather all of his courage and dignity. "I've already said that bit."

"Oh, yes," said the colossal, squeaky voice. "It's you again, Frank. Weren't you here quite recently?"

"It was forty years ago!" Dad shouted. "I was a young man then."

"How short are your human life spans. How pathetically short they are. Yes, I remember now," squeaked the voice.

"You came here asking me to grant special powers to that nasty little puppet of yours. So you could become the most famous puppeteer the world has ever known."

"That's right," replied Dad, looking shamefaced.

"Well," said the voice.

"Well, what?"

"Did you have a nice time?"

There was a pause.

"No!" said Dad. "It was awful!"

"Oh," said the voice.

"And . . . and we'd like you to take the nasty puppet back with you."

"Back with me?"

"Yes!" cried Dad. "He's evil!"

"Oh," said the voice. "I'm not sure I'm very keen on that idea."

Suddenly Tolstoy was shouting. He had stopped cowering away. He was swishing his wings and sneering at them both. "Don't listen to that old madman! I don't want to go anywhere. I'm quite happy here on Earth. I've got a new master and everything."

"Is this true, Tolstoy?" the voice squeaked.

"Yes! This boy. This Jason. I am going to make him a star, using the special powers you granted me."

"And this boy, this Jason, does he want to be a puppeteer? Have you asked him?"

"Of course he does." Tolstoy cackled. "Anyone would want such a destiny. I'm the greatest, longest-eared bat in the whole world!"

"And the nastiest," said the voice.

"Maybe . . ."

"And the wickedest . . ."

"Perhaps . . ."

"And the most ruthless."

"Well, what's that got to do with it?"

I blinked. While all this to and fro was going on, faces were materializing among the flames. It was like real magic and it took a few moments to focus on what was actually happening.

There were cries of fright and recognition from Mam and Barry and Lisa and the others. The shapes in the savage flames were coalescing and becoming brighter and then more distinct. They whirled and danced in the updraught of the flames.

"Here are your friends, Tolstoy," said the huge voice, making the whole forest shake.

Tolstoy was rigid. He stared at the dancing shapes and his glass eyes just about dropped out of his head.

No wonder. All of his victims were waiting for him in the inferno. Nixon the penguin, Toby the cheeky monkey,

Josephine the sea horse and then other, assorted, animals and
Tootles, drifting and swimming about.

"Come to us . . . come with us, Tolstoy . . . ," they wailed
in a ghostly chorus. "We want you, Tolstoy. We want you
with us. . . ."

Josephine the sea horse looked particularly frightening.

"Nooooo!" Tolstoy shrieked. "I won't go! I won't!"

"Ah," squeaked the huge voice. "I think you have no
choice in the matter."

Dad started shouting at me, across the space of melting
snow. "Take him off your hand, Jason! Chuck the bat into
the flames!"

I heard him.

But I hesitated.

Tolstoy was looking at me beseechingly. Great tears were
standing out in his eyes.

"Come with us!" cried his puppet victims.

Behind us I could hear Barry gagging and sobbing at the
sight of his spectral penguin.

"Don't make me go," whined Tolstoy. "Please, Jason.
Tell him you want me to stay . . . I'll be good. . . . I'll be
better . . ."

I stared at the flames, where more shapes were material-izing. We were starting to get a glimpse into the heart of puppet hell itself.

I couldn't say anything. I was frozen.

"Jason?" squeaked the voice. "Do you want him? If you say you want him now, you must keep him forever."

"I . . . ," I said. "I-I . . ."

One massive shape had appeared in the flames. A ghastly, leering face. A little body. I knew it was the owner of the huge and squeaky voice. We were all looking at the face of the Great One himself, and he was wearing a jester's hat. He had a chin and nose so long and pointed they almost met in the middle. He had narrow little eyes, alive with malice and glee. It was the king of puppets himself, familiar to me from seaside shows when I was a little kid. You'd see him doing his shows in stripy booths on a tiny stage. He had a wife and a baby and there was always a policeman and a crocodile involved, for some reason.

Something creepy about him. Something very old-fashioned. Mr. Punch. Mr. Punch was the king of puppet hell. The Great One himself.

He was waving his rolling pin about in the flames and his other little arm was whirling around a massive string of sausages.

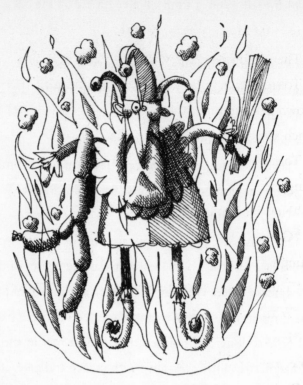

"Decide! You must decide!" the Great One cried in his shrill voice.

Tolstoy's eyes were wide and green. "Jason!"

I knew that everyone's eyes were on me. Tolstoy's. Mr. Punch's. My family's. Lisa's. They were all waiting.

I looked Tolstoy right in the eye.

"I never asked to be a puppeteer," I said.

And I wrenched him off my hand. "I don't know what I want to be."

I held him up by his tattered, sheeny wings. "And I don't know what I want to do with my life yet!"

Then I flung him away.

Tolstoy gave one last tortured, terrifying scream. I'd thrown him right into the heart of the flames. Right into Mr. Punch's crimson, laughing mouth.

Tolstoy was a whirling black shape, growing smaller: vanishing into the fiery vortex.

"Now," squeaked Mr. Punch, "I can go!"

"Good!" Dad shouted, grinning. His face was shining in triumph. "Thank you, Great One."

"There's just one more thing," said Mr. Punch.

"What's that?" asked Dad.

"I want to remind you of the terms of our bargain, all those years ago."

Dad's head jerked in sudden fear. "What?"

Mr. Punch howled with mirth. "That's right, Frank Lurcher! That's the way to do it! That's the way to do it!"

Dad was backing away in horror.

"What is it, Dad?" I cried, running to him through the melting snow.

"Tolstoy isn't enough!" Dad gibbered. "He wants to take me as well! Jason! He wants to take me!"

"Frank!" Mam moaned. "Frank! Don't leave me!"

We watched then as my dad was dragged by some invisible force onto his knees in the slushy snow. He cried out as he struggled against these unseen forces, but it was no good.

He was sliding backwards into the fiery pit.

My mam was shrieking now. She didn't want him to go. After all their fights, after all the misery and moods, she still didn't really want him to go to hell.

"Help me!" Dad howled. "HELP ME!"

There was nothing any of us could do. Dad had made his bargain, all those years ago. He was back in his senses. He'd saved me from Tolstoy. But there was nothing at all I could do to help him.

Mr. Punch was squeaking in that profound, earth-shattering voice, "That's the way to do it! That's the way to do it! Come along, Frank! It's time to go home!"

"GAAAAGGGGHHH!" screeched my dad as Mr. Punch's string of sausages whipped out and bound him like chains. He fell into the flames at last and Mr. Punch's fat wooden hands clamped hold of him.

"Good-bye, everybody!" the Great One screeched. "We're going now! Good-bye! Good-bye!"

And then the gateway closed and the lights went out and the rest of us were left in the wintry woods.

Epilogue

The Good, the Bat, and the Ugly

by Jason Lurcher

256 pp published June 2004

Mamazon ranking: 4,888,987

SUMMARY

Small boy is given lovely puppet by parents and it goes round killing people. True story.

Mamazon REVIEW

Following a recent trend in celebrity-offspring auto-biographies comes thirteen-year-old Jason Lurcher's alarming memoir, *The Good, the Bat, and the Ugly*. This young author brings us the tale of how his (not-so) famous father came to mysteriously disappear at the end of last year. We don't want to spoil the ending, but is any of this very likely? These are just puppets! They only PRETEND to talk! Come on! They're just fur and fabric with someone's hand inside! How is the reading public supposed to accept any of this as TRUE FACT? What's more, this odd little book is aimed at a youth market. A KIDDIE'S book. It's too nasty for them. Violent and horrible, with swearing in. And the devil. Children really want lovely fantasy with nice magic and characters they can BELIEVE IN.

FROM THE PUBLISHER

An extremely brave young man and upcoming author, Jason Lurcher has been trapped from an early age in a world of evil puppets gone mad. Here, for the first time, he tells his own harrowing tale! Told with tenderness, delicacy and amazing sensitivity, *The Good, the Bat, and the Ugly* will alert the world to the dreadful dangers of glove puppetry.

REVIEW BY LISA TURMOIL,
HAIRSTYLIST TO THE STARS
***** *FIVE STARS. I WAS THERE! IT'S ALL TRUE!!!*

I don't know what that first review was on about. I was there and I know it's all true, so he can just get his own facts right and shut up. Jason Lurcher tells nothing but the truth about the awful time we had when he was taken over by Tolstoy and everything. I hope they make a big Hollywood film of it and I get to play the part of me or at least style all the stars' hair for it. It was me who told Jason to write the book in the first place, to help him get over his dad going to hell and all, and while his mam was off making herself into a big TV star like she is now. Anyway I'm fill-ing up all the space, but well done, Jason, you're a real star even without a puppet and I'm proud of you. And thank you!!! For making me seem a lot slimmer in the book than I am in real life!!!

67 out of 68 customers found this review helpful.

REVIEW BY . . . B. LURCHER
* ONE STAR. NO ONE LIKES A SHOW-OFF!

You'll never be a millionaire (like me, your brother—if you've forgotten) by writing books like this. You're not too young to sue, you know. You're a heartless, callow young man. Authors have a great responsibility to tell the truth, you know. You've just made yourself look good and all the rest of us like right arses!! And that Lisa Turmoil is wrong about everything except her weight. She's about eighteen stone in real life.

3 out of 68 customers found this review helpful.

REVIEW BY MARJORIE STAYNES
** TWO STARS. A BIT FRIGHTENING.

Readers might be interested in reading my own book, JOSEPHINE AND ME: MY LIFE WITH A DARLING SEA HORSE. It's a much nicer read than Jason's book, all about poor, lovely Josephine, star of stage and screen, who met her tragic end.

0 out of 68 customers found this review helpful.

REVIEW BY . . . JASON'S MUMMY

****** FIVE STARS.*

BUT ONLY BECAUSE HE'S MY LITTLE BOY.

I'm really, really famous now, as everyone knows, for my appearances on daytime television, so it's not like we really need the money. He wouldn't show his mummy what he was writing until it was published. Oh, Jason—how could you? I'd just like to tell everyone that he has always had a fanciful imagination and that we didn't all run around like idiots and that "maniacs" and "loonies" are awful things to call people and that the devil didn't appear to us. Jason has written a whole lot of fantastical nonsense that came out of his silly head. As his darling mummy, I know that the poor boy has been under a lot of stress, what with his daddy disappearing and everything. Anyway—I hope if there's a big Hollywood blockbuster made about it that I'm in it too. I'd be very good in it, playing myself. I don't think Lisa Turmoil would, though. They'd need someone more petite.

3 out of 68 customers found this review helpful.

REVIEW BY TOLSTOY THE LONG-EARED BAT
***** *FIVE STARS. HAHAHAHAHAHAHAHAHAHA-*
HAHAHAHAHAHA

DID YOU THINK I'D GONE FOR GOOD? DID YOU THINK THAT WAS AN END TO IT? I TOLD HIM WE WERE BOUND TOGETHER FOR LIFE. HE DOESN'T KNOW WHAT IT'S REALLY LIKE, OWNING A PUPPET. YOU DON'T GET AWAY AS EASILY AS ALL THAT!

68 out of 68 customers found this review helpful.